ULTIMATUM

Sheriff Reynolds opened his mouth to speak, then looked around the saloon, noticing that they were the center of attention. He sat down at Clint's table, and lowered his voice. "You and the old man have until tomorrow morning to leave town."

"We haven't broken any laws," Clint said. "You can't run us out of town."

"Sure I can," Reynolds said. "You've broken one of *my* laws."

"Which law is that, Sheriff?"

Reynolds leaned forward and said, "You tried to make me look like a fool in my own town. I don't stand for that. It's in your best interest to leave by tomorrow morning."

"I'll consider it."

"Do more than that, mister," Reynolds said. "Do a helluva lot more than that."

* * *

SPECIAL PREVIEW!

Turn to the back of this book for a special excerpt from an exciting new western . . .

Gunpoint

. . . the shattering story of a deadly blood feud by America's new star of the classic western, Giles Tippette.

DON'T MISS THESE
ALL-ACTION WESTERN SERIES
FROM THE BERKLEY PUBLISHING GROUP

***THE GUNSMITH* by J. R. Roberts**
Clint Adams was a legend among lawmen, outlaws, and ladies. They called him . . . the Gunsmith.

***LONGARM* by Tabor Evans**
The popular long-running series about U.S. Deputy Marshal Long—his life, his loves, his fight for justice.

***LONE STAR* by Wesley Ellis**
The blazing adventures of Jessica Starbuck and the martial arts master, Ki. Over eight million copies in print.

***SLOCUM* by Jake Logan**
Today's longest-running action western. John Slocum rides a deadly trail of hot blood and cold steel.

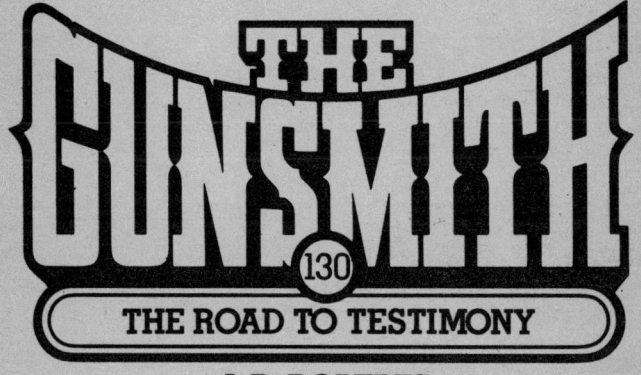

THE ROAD TO TESTIMONY

J. R. ROBERTS

JOVE BOOKS, NEW YORK

THE ROAD TO TESTIMONY

A Jove Book / published by arrangement with
the author

PRINTING HISTORY
Jove edition / October 1992

All rights reserved.
Copyright © 1992 by Robert J. Randisi.
Gunpoint excerpt copyright © 1992 by Giles Tippette.
This book may not be reproduced in whole
or in part, by mimeograph or any other means,
without permission. For information address:
The Berkley Publishing Group,
200 Madison Avenue,
New York, New York 10016.

ISBN: 0-515-10957-6

Jove Books are published by The Berkley Publishing Group,
200 Madison Avenue, New York, New York 10016.
The name "JOVE" and the "J" logo
are trademarks belonging to Jove Publications, Inc.

PRINTED IN THE UNITED STATES OF AMERICA

10 9 8 7 6 5 4 3 2 1

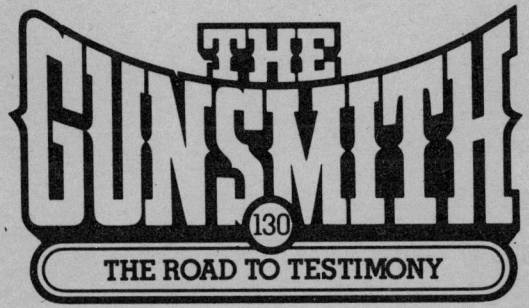

ONE

Being bushwhacked was not a new experience for Clint Adams, but that didn't make it any easier for him to take. He dropped from the saddle at the sound of the first shot and rolled into a gully. His big black gelding, Duke, ran off to safety, which suited Clint fine.

Now came the waiting. This was the part Clint hated the most. He knew he could use the time to try to figure out just how many bushwhackers there were, but it was still a pain in the butt to have to lie in a gully—or a dry wash, or behind a bush, or whatever cover he took at that particular time— and wait.

To pass the time, Clint tried to count the times he had been bushwhacked in the past twenty years or so. There was the time outside of Reno . . . the time in California, when he was with . . . who was he with, McIntyre? . . . and then the time near Denver. . . .

He'd been bushwhacked by one man, two men, a man and a woman, two men and a woman, two white men and an Indian . . . or was that one white man and two Indians?

"Jesus," he said, looking up at the sky. How long had he been here this time?

He rolled over, took off his hat, placed it on the barrel of his gun, and raised it just high enough to draw fire. Several shots were fired, enough to tell him that there were at least three bushwhackers. He brought the hat down and found one hole. At least one of them could shoot, then, he thought as he put the hat back on.

He looked at the sky again. The sun was still high, and there would be daylight for hours yet. He couldn't sit here in this gully that long, not without water. He was going to have to do something to draw them out . . . whoever *they* were. . . .

"What are we waiting for, Wheat?" Del Beman asked.

"Wheat" was Bill Wheaton, who was calling the shots on this ambush.

With Beman and Wheat were Dick Wheeler and Rich House, both perfectly willing to follow either Beman or Wheat. Wheeler and House were born followers, while Beman and Wheat often came to blows over who the leader of the four should be.

In this case it was Wheat, because it was he who had recognized the Gunsmith back in Dogtown, Wyoming.

"We're waitin' him out," Wheat said. He was a tall, slender, handsome man in his late twenties. In fact, all four were the same approximate age, having grown up together. Wheat was generally considered the handsome one, while Beman was thought of as the smart one. Of course, Wheat argued that, and Beman didn't think that Wheat was all *that* much better-looking than he. Wheeler and House were both homely, and dumb as fence posts. Wheeler was well over six feet and gangly, while House was about five-six and scrawny.

"Yeah? Well, how long are we gonna do that?" Beman asked. He was a little shorter than Wheat, which bothered him, but he was heavier, filled out a bit more through the chest and shoulders. "Hell, we got better'n ten thousand dollars out of the Dogtown Bank, and here we are just a few miles from town.

THE ROAD TO TESTIMONY

There's probably a whole damn posse out lookin' for us."

"Del," Wheaton said, "we checked that town out before we hit the bank, remember? They got an old sheriff and a kid deputy. We gotta worry about a posse out of Dogtown, we better hang up our guns and become farmers."

"Yeah, well," Beman said, "I still wonder what that bank was doin' with ten thousand dollars in it."

"There's a lot of people in and around Dogtown who put their hard-earned money into that bank," Wheat said, and then added, "Lucky for us."

"Wheat?" House said.

"What?"

"Tell us again who this feller is?"

Wheeler nodded his agreement. He wanted it explained again, too.

"They call him the Gunsmith, you idiot!" Wheat said impatiently. "Ain't you ever heard of the Gunsmith?"

"Sure, Wheat," House said, nodding. "I heard of him."

"He's good with a gun," Wheeler said.

"Very good, Dick," Wheat said sarcastically.

"And we're gonna kill him?" House asked, frowning. That was the part that confused him. If the Gunsmith was so good with a gun, how were they going to kill him?

"Yeah, we are," Wheat said.

"How?" Wheeler asked.

"There's four of us, Dick," Wheat said. "That's how."

"Well," Beman said, "there's only gonna be three of you if we don't move pretty soon. I still don't like bein' this close to a town where we just robbed the bank."

"And killed a teller," Wheeler pointed out. Wheaton gave him a hard look, and he subsided sheepishly.

"All right, then," Wheat said. "If you're so all-fired worried about the law from a place called Dogtown, we'll do something."

"Like what?" Beman asked.

"Like talk to him."

"Is that all?" House asked.

"No," Wheat said, "that's not all. Now listen, all of you . . ."

"Hey, Gunsmith?"

It's about time, Clint thought. Bushwhackers usually liked to talk to their victims, but these fellers had taken their sweet time getting to this point in the festivities.

"I hear you!" Clint called back.

"We got you outnumbered," the voice called. "Why don't you come on out and face us?"

"All of you?"

"Hey," the voice said. "There's only two of us. Feller with your rep, that shouldn't be such bad odds."

He was lying. There were at least three of them; that's what Clint had figured from the shots fired earlier.

"You're willing to play the odds, though, that right?" Clint called.

"Hell," the voice said. "I think I can take you myself, but my friend here wants a piece of you, too."

Sure, Clint thought, that's why they bushwhacked him, because each thought they could take him alone.

"I tell you what," Clint said. "Why don't you step out and I'll face you one at a time."

There was a long silence, and then the voice said something Clint wasn't expecting to hear.

"All right," the voice called out. "You got a deal."

Obviously they were agreeing so they could try something.

"There are conditions!" Clint called.

"Name 'em."

"One man stands out, the other two stand where I can see them," Clint said. In his mind he had settled on three men.

"The others won't lay their guns down," the voice called.

"As long as their hands are where I can see them," Clint said.

There was a period of silence—designed to make him think that *they* were thinking the terms over—and then the voice said, "All right, we agree."

"Let's do it, then," Clint said.

He peered out from his cover and saw three men. One was very tall, one short, the third medium height, slenderly built. Clint pegged the slender, medium-built one as the spokesman.

He stood up as the tall and short one stepped away, keeping their hands away from their sides. It appeared that the speaker was going to try him first.

He stepped out of the gully while the other man took a few steps forward.

"What's your name?" Clint asked.

"What's that matter?" the man replied.

Clint was about to answer when he realized that he had made a grave error. I'm getting old, he thought, and I just might not get any older because of it. . . .

There was a shot, and he felt the pain in his center of his back.

TWO

Snatches of conversation, drifting in and out . . .
"Whatta we do now?"
"Let's ride . . . he's dead . . ."
" . . . did it?"
"Yeah, House . . . we did it . . ."
Men's voices, fading away . . .

"Lordy . . . done got yerself shot up good, dint ya. . . ."
A woman's voice, close to him.
" . . . see if we kin get you on ol' Suzie . . ."
He was being dragged, and lifted, and couldn't move to help.
" . . . is he, Doc?"
"Damned lucky . . . missed his spine . . . could have been worse . . ."
A man and a woman, close by, but fading in and out . . .
"How long . . . ?"
" . . . quite some time, Liz . . ."
" . . . got nothin' better to do . . ."
"Me neither . . ."

THE ROAD TO TESTIMONY

• • •

"You're awake."

Clint opened his eyes and looked up. He realized that he was lying on his side, and there seemed to be pillows behind him, keeping him propped that way. Things were a little hazy, but hovering above him he could see a face, a woman's face that had seen some hard living but was still not unattractive. Tanned, lined face, nice eyes, good mouth . . .

"You are awake, ain't ya?"

He frowned and said, "I think so."

"Let's see how long this time."

"What do you mean?"

"You keep wakin' up and goin' to sleep on me," she said. "An' when you wake up again, you don't remember bein' awake before. I keep havin' to tell you the same things over and over again."

"I'm sorry—"

"Don't apologize," she said. "Lord knows you should be dead. Leastways, that's what the doc said."

"A doctor," he said. "I think I remember hearing a doctor."

"What'd you hear?"

"Can't remember much," Clint said. "Something about my spine . . ." It occurred to Clint then that he couldn't feel his legs. He tried to move them and had no success. "I can't feel . . . or move . . . my legs."

"Doc says you was lucky," she said. "The bullet missed yer spine."

"Why can't I feel . . ."

"He said something about the swelling," she said. "Bullet came close, and the swelling might be pressing on yer spine. When the swelling goes down he says you should be able to move."

"And walk?"

"I guess," she said, shrugging.

Clint moved his hand—and was glad he could—and rubbed his face. He felt no whiskers or stubble.

"You been shaving me?"

"And cleaning you," she said. She saw the look on his face and added, "Don't worry, mister. You ain't got nothin' I ain't already seen."

"I'm grateful to you," he said. "How did you get me here?"

"Hoisted you up onto ol' Suzie and walked you back."

"Ol' Suzie . . . is a horse?"

"A mule."

"And you lifted me up onto her back . . . alone?"

"I may not be much to look at, but I'm pretty strong," she said. "You gonna stay awake on me this time?"

Clint frowned. The haziness had left, and his eyesight seemed pretty clear.

"I think so."

"Feel like eatin' somethin'?"

"Not really."

"I'm gonna feed you some soup, anyway," she said, standing up. It was only then he realized she had been sitting. She was a tall woman, angularly built. "Doc says I gotta feed you to keep you alive."

"When will the doctor be back?" he asked.

"Soon."

"What's soon?"

"Three, maybe four days. 'Sakes, he was here a week ago."

"That long?"

"He's the only doc around here, and it takes him time to get around. Yer a star patient of his, or so he says. Maybe he'll be back sooner. He's sure interested in how yer doin'."

"Glad to hear it."

"I'm gonna get that soup," she said. "You stay where you are, hear?"

Jesus, he thought, she's got a sense of humor.

THREE

The soup was hot.

"I never said I was a great cook," she said in her own defense. She set the empty bowl down on the table near the bed.

"It was fine," he said. "Thanks."

He started looking around and she asked, "What're ya lookin' for?"

"My gun."

"I got it."

"Could you put it where I can reach it... please?" he asked.

"Who you plannin' on shootin'?"

"I'm not planning on shooting anyone," he said, and then added to himself, not yet.

"Then you don't needs yer gun, do ya?"

"Yes," he said. "I do."

She tried to stare him down, and when she couldn't she shrugged and said, "Ain't no skin off my butt."

She got up, walked out of his view, and when she returned she was carrying his gunbelt.

"Just hang it on the bedpost," he said. She did, and he reached up and touched it, although the move caused him some pain in his back.

"Back hurt?"

"Yes."

"Doc says that's good."

"It's not *his* back," Clint said, but he knew what she meant. If he *couldn't* feel any pain, that would be a bad sign.

"I got work to do," she said, picking up the empty soup bowl and heading for the door.

"Hey."

"Yeah?"

"Am I in your bed?"

"You are," she said, "but don't let it worry you none. I got me a nice comfortable chair out here."

Before he could say anything else, she was gone. Moments later, he was asleep.

The next time he woke up he was pleased to find that it was still the same day—although evening—and he remembered everything the woman had told him . . . except maybe her name.

After she finished feeding him some more soup he asked, "Have we exchanged names?"

"Ain't hardly had the time," she said. "Mine's Liz Burke— Elizabeth, that is, but you kin call me Liz."

"Liz, my name's Clint Adams."

She stared at him for a moment, and although there was no flicker in her eyes he was sure she had recognized the name.

"Glad to meet you," she said. She grabbed the bowl and started to leave the room.

"Excuse me."

"Yeah?"

"My horse," he said. "Have you seen him?"

"A big black gelding?"

"That's him."

"That beast wandered in here the day after I found you," she said. "He was hungry, so I fed him. I been caring for him since."

"I thank you for that."

"Don't thank me," she said. "Be a sin not to take care of an animal like that." She left the room before he could say anything else.

Now that she knew who he was, he wondered what she was going to do. She couldn't very well kick him out, not while he couldn't walk. Still, she was going to have to wonder what she had stepped into.

He couldn't very well worry about that when he had to worry about whether he'd ever walk again. She'd have to deal with it the best she could, and if she asked for help, he'd give her whatever help he could. He himself didn't think that the bushwhackers would be back. They'd shot him in the back, left him for dead, and figured they were done with him.

They didn't know just how wrong they were, and he was going to walk again if only to show them.

Liz came into the room later that night and obviously thought he was asleep. She didn't turn up the light when she approached the bed. He cracked his eyes and in the dark could see her silhouette, although he couldn't make out the expression on her face. He felt her hand touch his hair, her fingers fiddling with it for a few moments, then trail down across his face. Her hand was rough, but her touch was gentle. Finally she used both hands to cover him well with the sheet and blanket, and then she turned and left. He was glad he hadn't let her know he was awake; she might have been embarrassed.

It was bad enough that she seemed lonely without being embarrassed as well.

● ● ●

In the other room of the two-room cabin that Liz Burke had built herself she tried to get comfortable in her chair, but thoughts of the man in the other room kept her from falling asleep. Instead, she closed her eyes and thought of the times she had cleaned him while he was unconscious. She dwelled on that particular time where, while she had him naked and was washing him with a cloth, he had become erect. Liz Burke had lived alone a long time, and had not been with a man for almost that long. To have a man in her bed, naked, attractive, beautifully erect and—dammit—unconscious had been too much for her to bear. Her cheeks burned as she recalled how she had leaned over him and pressed her cheek to his erection. How she had become even bolder and took hold of him with her hand, enjoying the smooth feel of him, the heat of him, how she had cupped his testicles in her hand, and finally how she had opened her mouth and taken him inside.

She had lost control of herself then, her head bobbing up and down on the unconscious man until, even in that state, he had lifted his hips and moaned as he exploded into her mouth. For that one moment it had been a glorious experience, but when it was over she had cleaned him and fled the room in shame.

Now she felt herself growing excited, moist between her legs, her nipples erect, and she knew that before he left she was going to have to have him inside of her. The only problem was, she knew what she looked like, and once he was well he'd be on his way. There would be no way she could convince him to lay with her before he left.

She was afraid that it wouldn't happen unless she could catch him asleep and helpless . . . again.

FOUR

Ten days after he awoke for good, the doctor returned to examine him again. He introduced himself as Dr. Ben Miller. He was a tall, well-built man in his late thirties.

As the doctor undressed him, Clint looked over at Liz, who was still in the room, and the doctor caught the look.

"Mr. Adams, she's cleaned and bathed you for weeks, and has been in the room every time I've examined you. It would be a little silly to become modest now."

Clint smiled and said, "I know, Doc."

Clint felt some pain when the doctor turned him over to examine his back, and then more when the doctor probed the area of the wound.

When he was finished, the doctor turned him back over onto his side.

"What's the verdict, Doc?"

"Well, the swelling seems to be subsiding. Do you have any feeling in your legs yet?"

"No, not yet."

"Hmm," the doctor said.

"What's that mean?"

"There's still plenty of time," the doctor said. "The swelling still has a ways to go before it subsides completely, but I believe you will regain the feeling in your legs."

"And complete movement?"

"Well . . . that might be up to you, Mr. Adams."

"Meaning what?"

"Meaning that you aren't going to be able to simply stand up and walk at any stage," Dr. Miller explained. "It's going to take time, and you'll have to do it gradually. It might almost be like learning to walk all over again."

"If that's what I have to do, Doc," Clint said, "I'll do it."

"Not alone you won't."

"If I have to."

"He won't have to," Liz said.

The doctor looked at her and said, "Do you know what you'll be taking on, Liz?"

"Ain't got a hell of a lot else to do, Doc, do I?" Liz said. "I got too much time invested in him already, anyway. Be a shame not to see it through."

"Liz—" Clint started, but the doctor cut him off.

"Forget it, Mr. Adams," he said. "I've seen that stubborn look on Liz's face too many times before. She's going to help you whether you want her to or not."

"Well," Clint said, "I'm certainly not going to turn down her help, that's for sure."

"Then it's settled," the doc said, starting to pack up his little black bag. "I should be back through this way sometime next month."

"Should I have the feeling back in my legs by then?" Clint asked.

The doctor gave him the kind of smile Clint was sure doctors practiced and said, "We'll see about that, won't we?"

"Oh, and Doc?" Clint said. "Let's keep my identity quiet."

The doc nodded and then Liz walked him out, and Clint

spent the next few minutes trying to will the feeling back into his legs. He was trying to lift them, and was covered with perspiration by the time Liz reentered the room.

"What are you tryin' to do?" she demanded.

"Move."

"Any luck?"

He stopped trying and stared at her.

"No."

She wrinkled her nose and said, "You're all sweated up. I'll have to wash you."

"You don't have to."

"I ain't gonna have you stinkin' up my house, Clint Adams," she said. "I'll get the basin and cloth."

The first time she had washed him—the first time while he was *awake*—it had made him extremely uncomfortable. He had bathed with women before, but that was when they were both enjoying it. He had never *been* bathed by a woman before, when he was nearly helpless. The second time wasn't as bad, and after that he got kind of used to it.

The last time, however, a couple of days earlier, he had noticed something. Maybe it was his imagination, but there was something in Liz Burke's touch that day that was different. She was not as workmanlike as she had been in the past when washing him, and she had been hesitant when handing him the cloth so he could wash his private parts. He *knew* that she had washed his penis and testicles while he was unconscious, but while he was awake she was letting him do that himself.

When she entered the room he remained silent while she set the basin and cloth down and then turned down the sheet, uncovering him. He was still naked from the doctor's examination. She wet the cloth and washed his chest and shoulders, his arms and underarms, his neck. After that she did his feet and legs and thighs, which he could not feel. She did not do his genitals, but turned him onto his other side so she could do his back, the backs of his legs, and then his buttocks. It seemed to him that she took longer over his buttocks than she usually did, but once again it could have been his imagination.

What wasn't his imagination was the erection he had when she turned him back over. He couldn't help it. It had come unbidden while she had been washing his buttocks. It was probably the first time he had really thought of her as a woman—and as a woman she wasn't unattractive. In fact, he probably would have called her handsome, and she was certainly attractive to the doctor. Clint was sure the man was sweet on her, only she was so sure she was unattractive that she wouldn't have noticed.

"Liz—"

"Here," she said, handing him the cloth and then averting her eyes, "you'd better—"

"No," he said. "You do it."

"What?" she said, staring at him.

"I'd like you to."

She stared at him a little longer, then gingerly applied the cloth, first to his testicles, holding them in one hand and washing them with the other. After that she closed her hand—which was inside the cloth—over him and began to rub him. He may have had no feeling in his legs, but he certainly had feeling *there*.

He moaned, and she looked at him and then boldly began running her hand up and down him faster, biting her bottom lip. He reached for her then, and slid his hand inside the gapped neck of her plain dress. She gasped as he palmed her breasts, which were small but surprisingly round and firm. Her nipples were hard, and as he tweaked them she abandoned the pretense of the cloth, letting it fall away so that he was in her bare hand.

"Clint—" she said huskily.

He leaned to his right so he could reach her with the other hand as well, placing it on the back of her neck while he continued to massage her breast with his left. He had intended to apply a little pressure, bending her head down to him, but he didn't have a chance. She lowered her head herself, and then he felt her lips and tongue on him.

"Oh, God," she said against him. "It's been so long. . . ."

"Liz . . ." he said, rubbing his hand on the back of her neck. With his left hand he undid the buttons on the front of her dress, then used both hands to pull it down from her shoulders.

She straightened then, grasping the dress with both hands before it could fall to her waist.

"Clint—" she said.

"I want to see you, Liz," he said. "Please, let me see you."

She stared at him, her eyes liquid, and then she removed her hands so that the dress fell to her waist.

"Come here," he said. "Come closer, where I can see you. . . ."

She moved closer to him and he palmed both of her breasts, which were white and firm, while the rest of her was dark brown from the sun.

He put an arm around her and drew her down to him so he could kiss her breasts and lick her nipples. She moaned, sliding her hand down through his pubic hair until she had ahold of him again. He bit her nipples while her hand pumped him. Then he kissed her neck, and brought her thin lips to his. They were resistant at first, and then they softened, her tongue blossoming in his mouth, sweeter than he might have thought. He tasted whiskey on her tongue, also, which might explain why they were finally doing what they were doing.

She moaned into his mouth, then pulled away and began to kiss his chest, his belly, sliding her tongue over him, through his pubic hair until her mouth swooped down on him and took him inside. Her head bobbed up and down as she sucked him wetly, her head moving faster and faster. He wanted to use his legs to lift himself off the bed, but he couldn't, so he grasped her head and just held on until finally he groaned aloud and exploded.

From that day on they did everything but truly have sex. He wanted her to straddle him, but she was afraid of hurting him.

"We'll have time," she would say, "when you're well, before you leave . . ."

Clint was grateful that she was the one who spoke of his leaving, making it clear that she expected him to.

One night, a few weeks after that first day, he told her to get into bed with him.

"Your back—"

"I won't feel any pain, having you in bed with me," he said. "I want your lovely body next to me."

"It's not," she said.

"What?"

"It's not lovely—"

"Of course it is," he said. "What kind of nonsense is that?"

"I'm scrawny," she said, "and my skin is—"

"Smooth and wonderful," he said.

"Look," she said, showing him the rough skin of her hands.

He took her hands in his and kissed them.

"That's from hard work," he said, "and nothing to be afraid of. How old are you, Liz, thirty-nine?"

Her eyes flickered and she said, "I'm forty."

She looked forty-five—at least her face and hands did. The rest of her was marvelous, strong, sinewy, smooth skin, and he told her so.

"Come on," he said, "lay with me."

She relented and got into bed with him. He put his arm around her and drew her close. She was tentative at first, then put her head on his shoulder and pressed herself against him. Her body was hot, as was her breath on his neck. In moments she was asleep, and from that day on she slept with him.

FIVE

"Ouch."

Liz looked up quickly at Clint and said, "Did I hurt you?"

"Damn right you did!"

"I'm sorry—"

"You hurt my leg."

She paused a moment, then said, "What?"

"You leaned on my right leg," he said, "and it hurt."

She looked down at his leg, frowned, and then reached out and pinched him.

"Ouch," he said again, and then she fell into his arms and he began to laugh and she began to cry. Forgotten was his erection—which she had been working on rather energetically with her mouth, and which was now deflating.

After they had both regained their composure she asked, "Can you move?"

He tried but could not. Still, he refused to be discouraged.

"At least I can *feel*," he said, "and that's a beginning."

"It sure is," she said.

She looked down at his penis, which was now semierect, and then leaned over and kissed it. Immediately it began to rise to the occasion and she smiled at him and said, "Time to celebrate."

When the doctor returned and heard the good news he was almost as happy as they had been. Clint could also tell from the man's face that he had already guessed where the relationship had gone.

The doctor examined Clint, and when he probed the wound he said, "Yes, the swelling has gone down considerably."

"When do you think I'll be able to move my legs, Doc?" Clint asked.

"Fairly soon, I'd say."

"And when can I sit a horse?"

"Oh, not for some time," the doctor said. "Why, are you anxious to?"

"Very anxious."

"Why—oh, I see. You want to ride into town to talk to the sheriff."

"Why would I want to do that?"

"To report what happened to you. I mean, I've told him, but he'd still like to hear it from you."

"Well, I'll be riding into town, Doc, but not to make any report."

"Then why?"

"He wants to go after them," Liz said. "The yahoos that shot him. He wants to go after them, and he thinks he'll get some information in town."

The doctor looked at Clint and said, "You don't want to let the law handle it?"

"No way, Doc," Clint said. "I'm the one who was backshot, and I'm the one who'll handle it."

"Well," the doctor said, closing his bag, "that's up to you, of course. But I warn you, you won't be going anywhere for some time yet."

"That's all right," Clint said. "*When* I do it isn't important, just *that* I do it."

The doctor looked at Liz, who just shrugged.

"Walk me out," he said to her.

"I'll be right back," she said to Clint.

When Liz came back into the room Clint said, "He likes you, you know."

"What?" she asked, frowning.

"The doctor—he's sweet on you."

"Yer crazy!"

"I don't think so, Liz," Clint said. "Pay attention next time you see him."

"He's younger than me."

"So what? What is he, thirty-four, thirty-five? That hardly matters."

"I still think yer crazy."

"I'm just telling you what I see."

"Yer still dizzy."

"I'm seeing things pretty clear, Liz."

"Like goin' after the men who shot you? Is that what you call thinkin' clear?" she demanded.

"Very clearly," Clint said. "By now they will have spread the word that I'm dead. They'll never expect me to come after them."

"Then don't."

"Why not?"

"Because if yer dead, you can stay dead. Forget about bein' the Gunsmith—oh, yeah, I recognized your name when you told me. I know who you are—or who you were. Don't you ever get tired of livin' up to a reputation?"

"So tired that I stopped trying," Clint said. "But I also stopped trying to deny it. It's a reputation that's about half deserved, if that, but it's mine, and I have to live with it."

"Not anymore," she said. "Not if everyone believes yer dead."

"Liz—"

"I'm not sayin' that you should stay here, Clint," she said hurriedly. "Go someplace else, be somebody else for a change."

"I tried that once," he said. "It didn't work. I'm sorry, Liz, but this is something I have to do."

"Yer gonna get yerself killed," she said. "How many were there? Three?"

He made a face and said, "Four. The fourth one's the one who backshot me."

"That doesn't make a difference, though, does it?" she asked. "Yer gonna make all four of them pay, aren't you?"

"That's right," Clint said.

"Give me one good reason why," she said. "Some reason that I can understand."

He hesitated a moment, then said, "I had a dream last night. A bad one. I jerked awake and didn't wake you, but I couldn't get back to sleep after that."

She remained silent, listening.

"I had a good friend once, a man with a big reputation. His name was Hickok."

She knew the name, of course, but didn't comment.

"You know how he was killed, right?"

Her mouth jerked and then she said, "He was shot in the back."

"That's right," Clint said, "shot in the back. I reacted badly to that at the time, and ever since then that's been my bad dream, sleeping or waking. Being killed from behind by some coward who couldn't face me. It almost happened this time, Liz. I can't just forget that . . . can I?"

This time she hesitated, and then she said, "No, I guess not."

She moved toward the door and asked, "Do you want some soup?"

"Sure," he said, "let's have some soup."

She nodded and left, and Clint folded his arms across his chest and shivered. He thought he had reacted pretty well to the dream, but now he realized that voicing it had only increased its effect.

Now that the feeling was returning to his legs he knew he'd be walking soon—well, maybe not *that* soon—and then, after that, back in the saddle. He could only hope that the trail wouldn't be completely cold by then.

SIX

A month later Clint stood on the porch—or what passed for a porch—outside of Liz's cabin. He leaned his weight on a cane that the doctor had brought him on his last visit. He'd only been on his feet a week, but he thought that tomorrow he might try hobbling around without the cane.

His back was stiff and sore, and the doctor said that would last for a while. The wound might even be affected in the future by weather change, but Clint knew about that already. He'd collected his fair share of wounds in the past, and he knew the aches and pains that came with them. He wasn't worried about that. His only worry was getting back in the saddle again.

Thoughts of the saddle caused him to take a walk to Liz's small barn. Inside he bypassed her plow horse and her mule and went to the stall where Duke was standing.

"How you doing, big boy?" he asked. He didn't touch the big animal, just admired him. Duke was a long ways from being a colt, but his glossy black coat still shone like one. He could also run into the ground any horse more than half his age. He was and always would be a remarkable animal, one who seemed to have found a fountain of youth.

"Clint?"

He turned at the sound of Liz's voice.

"You've taken good care of him," Clint said. "Of both of us, for that matter."

"You shouldn't walk so far from the house," she said. "At least not without your gun."

"Why not?" he said. "You saw the newspaper the doc brought with him last time." The *Dogtown Gazette* had carried the story of the Gunsmith's death, which it had picked up from a larger, eastern paper. Clint wondered how many of his friends had seen the story and believed it. Rick Hartman in Labyrinth, Texas, probably *didn't* believe it, but the longer he went without hearing from Clint, the closer he'd come to doing so, finally.

"How long a ride is it into town?" he asked suddenly.

"A couple of hours. Why?"

He looked at her and said, "Take me in."

"What?"

"In the buckboard," he said, turning to face her.

"Clint, you can't stand that ride—"

"You must need supplies by now. You haven't been to town since you found me."

"The doc brings me some stuff, but yeah, I could do some shopping. Still—"

He reached out and grabbed her arm.

"Please, Liz. I've got to send some telegrams," he explained. "There are people who think I'm dead who should be told I'm not."

She frowned, bit her lip, and then agreed.

"On one condition."

"What's that?"

"If the trip becomes too much for you we'll stop and rest, and then start back."

"Deal."
"And you'll be honest?"
"Honey," he said, "if I'm in pain, you'll know it."
"Why don't I believe that?" she asked dubiously.

SEVEN

He did feel a lot of pain during the trip, but he was so happy to be out of bed and out of the cabin that he was able to withstand it. When they finally rode into Dogtown, it looked like San Francisco to him. In reality, it was a small town that would never get any bigger, but it seemed to know that about itself, so the people he saw walking the streets seemed pretty satisfied.

Clint managed to get himself down from the buckboard seat before Liz could come around and offer him help. That was important to him. He didn't want to seem *too* infirm. It might invite trouble. He would have liked to leave the cane in the buckboard, but he wasn't that sure of his balance. To help him with his balance, though, his gun was on his hip.

"What do you want to do?" she asked.

"You go and do your shopping," he said. "I'll find my way around."

"Alone? But—"

"I'll go to the telegraph office, and I'll even stop in and see the doc. How's that?"

She frowned and said, "Just stay out of trouble, Clint."

"I've been trying to do that all my life, Liz."

"That's not very encouraging."

THE ROAD TO TESTIMONY 29

"Go," he said.

Reluctantly, she left him and walked toward the general store.

Clint crossed the street to the saloon and went inside. He hadn't had a drink since he'd been shot, and he felt the need for one.

He had told Liz a week ago to stop shaving him, and so he had that week's growth on his face. He felt that would change his appearance enough to keep people from recognizing him too readily. That, and the weight loss he'd suffered. By the time he was ready to go hunting he hoped that the weight would be back, but by the same token, by that time, he would have a full beard, and longer hair. His plan was to let people go on believing he was dead—until he found the four men.

The saloon was small and nearly empty. There was one man seated at a table and another standing at the bar. The seated man had a black case at his feet, leading Clint to believe that he was a drummer. The man at the bar simply seemed to be a ranch hand, or a trail bum. Either way, he was covered with dust.

"Help ya?" the bartender asked.

"A whiskey," Clint said, "and a beer."

"Comin' up."

When both drinks were set in front of him he downed the whiskey with relish and then sipped the beer.

"You look like you needed that," the bartender said.

"I did."

"Another whiskey?"

"One's enough," Clint said, gesturing with the beer mug, "but let me finish this and I might have another."

"Couldn't help noticing the cane when you walked in," the man said.

"My own fault," Clint said. "Tripped over my own feet and sprained my back."

"Tough."

"Yeah."

His curiosity satisfied, the bartender turned to walk away.

"I heard there was a bank robbery here not long ago," Clint said.

The man stopped and looked at him.

"Depends on your idea of long or not long," the bartender said. "It's been over two months."

"They get away with much?"

"From what I heard, over ten thousand."

"Seems like a lot for a bank in a town this size to have on hand in one day."

"There ain't another bank for miles," the bartender said. "There ain't no big ranchers around, but a lot of people have their small accounts in there. It adds up. Luckily, they didn't try to get into the safe, just took what was at the windows."

"That was lucky. They ever catch them?"

"No."

"How many were there?"

The bartender turned and faced Clint.

"You ask a lot of questions for a stranger."

"Sorry," Clint said. "I'm curious." He raised the cane so the bartender could see it and said, "I figured you'd understand that."

The bartender allowed a sheepish grin to cross his face and said, "Yeah, okay. There were four men. It looked like one of them took a job as a teller for a few weeks, probably to case the bank."

"And the town," Clint said. "What about the law?"

"Not much to speak of," the bartender said. "The sheriff was in his sixties, and his deputy was still wet behind the ears."

"Was?"

"We got a new sheriff now. Sort of like closin' the barn door after the horse got away, you know?"

THE ROAD TO TESTIMONY

"What about the old sheriff? He still around?"

"He's around," the bartender said. "He's got a room at the rooming house at the far end of town. Spends his time sittin' on the front porch."

"And the deputy?"

"I hired him as a swamper here," the bartender said. "Suits his talents a lot better."

"What was the sheriff's name?"

"Moon," the bartender said. "Cole Moon."

The name shocked Clint. He'd heard of Cole Moon. The man had an excellent reputation as a lawman, but Clint hadn't heard anything about him in years. He was sad to admit it, but he'd assumed that the man was dead.

"I know," the bartender said, reading his face, "Moon had a big rep once; that's why we hired him. After the robbery, though, the town council figured we needed a younger man. We hired Tom Slater."

That name meant nothing to Clint.

"What was he before you made him sheriff?"

"He was our schoolteacher."

The bartender had stiffened a bit, as if he expected a remark. Clint was sure that the man was on the town council.

He tossed two bits on the bar and said, "Much obliged."

"What about that second beer?"

"I'll be back for it before I leave town," Clint said. "Can you tell me where the telegraph office is?"

"We got one," the man said, in defense of his small town. "Only one for miles, like the bank. It's out the door to the left, and a block down."

"Thanks."

The other two men in the place had never looked up from their drinks. Clint gave them each a look and then left the saloon.

EIGHT

On the way to the telegraph office Clint tried to compose a telegraph message to Rick Hartman in Labyrinth, Texas. He wanted to let his friend know that he was still alive, but he didn't want to sign his name over an open wire.

When he got there he worded a short message in such a way that only Hartman would know who it was from, and then sent it. He knew that Hartman would tell very few people, if any, that he was still alive. His friend would wait for him to reveal that himself.

After he left the telegraph office he looked over at the buckboard and saw that Liz wasn't there yet. He decided to walk to the end of town to see if Cole Moon was indeed sitting on the front porch.

As he approached the rooming house he spotted a man seated in a straight wooden chair, just staring ahead of him. He didn't seem to be looking *at* anything in particular—at least not anything that anyone else could see.

When Clint reached the porch and stepped onto it the man still didn't focus his eyes on him.

"Cole Moon?" Clint asked.

THE ROAD TO TESTIMONY 33

The old man moved his head slowly and looked directly at Clint.

"I used to be."

"What?"

"I said, I used to be Cole Moon."

"Well, who are you now?"

"Nobody," the old man said. "Just nobody. Now I'm just a dead man."

The Cole Moon Clint was looking at was certainly nothing like the man Clint had heard of for years. This man appeared to be in his sixties, pale and withered, seeming almost frail. His eyes were watery, and his lips almost bloodless. He had the longest fingers and biggest knuckles Clint had ever seen.

"You mind if I sit a while?" Clint asked.

"Why would you want to?"

"Well . . . I've got a bad back and could use the rest."

"Set, then. Don't make no never mind to me."

Clint pulled a chair over and sat about three feet from the man. From that distance he could smell the man, and the odor—while obviously from the fact that the man hadn't bathed in some time—was more one of despair.

"You used to be sheriff of this town, they tell me," Clint said.

The man grunted.

"And then the bank was robbed."

"Like that was my fault," Moon said. "I told the damned bank president to hire some security, but he wouldn't do it. Said it was a waste of money. Well, now there's ten thousand dollars of wasted money."

"Can I ask you a question?"

"Seems like you already have."

"Did you put together a posse and go after those robbers?"

Moon looked at Clint, his mouth grimly set.

"I tried," Moon finally said. "I couldn't get nobody to ride with me, except that fool boy they give me as a deputy, and he would have just got hisself—and probably me—killed."

"And they blamed you for that, too?"

"Damned sight easier than blamin' themselves, waren't it?" Moon asked. "Sure, they jest fired me and hired themselves a new sheriff—a *schoolteacher*—and that fixes everythin'."

"Except it doesn't get the money back."

"No, it don't."

"Seems to me that pretty much leaves the money up for grabs," Clint said. "I mean, if someone was to catch up to those robbers and take it off of them."

"That money's long gone and spent," Moon said. "That's the way of bank robbers."

"Usually."

Moon looked at Clint and asked, "You plannin' on goin' after them?"

"I am," Clint said, "but not for the money."

"Then why? You ain't from this town."

"No, I'm not," Clint said, "but I believe that the same men who robbed your bank backshot me and left me to die."

Moon stared at Clint for a few moments, as if trying to memorize his face, and then said, "I know you, don't I? I mean, without the whiskers and you probably wasn't always so skinny. I know you."

"Maybe you do."

"That's what's wrong with your back, huh?"

"That's right," Clint said. "One bullet, just missed my spine."

"You don't look like you're in any shape to go chasin' after anybody, let alone four men."

Clint tapped the porch floor with the cane and said, "No, not now, but pretty soon. When I do go after them, though, I might need some help."

The old man laughed, then coughed, hawked, and spat, and laughed again.

"You ain't gonna get anybody from here."

"I might," Clint said.

"Like who?"

"I need a good man," Clint said, "an experienced man."

"You ain't talkin' about me, are you?"

"I am."

"You're crazy."

"No, I'm not," Clint said. "As soon as I can sit a horse I'm going after them, even though I may not be in shape to take on four men."

"You'll get yourself killed."

"Maybe."

Moon stared at Clint again, then used the palms of his hands to wipe the mucus from his eyes and studied his face again.

"I know you."

"I'm like you, Moon," Clint said. "I'm a dead man."

"That's it!" Moon said, slapping his thigh. Clint was surprised that the thigh or the hand that struck it didn't snap like a twig. "I do know you. You're—"

"Shhh," Clint said, putting up his hand to silence the old man. "I'm dead, and I want to stay that way, at least for a while."

The old man looked around and said in a lowered voice, "I understand."

"I tell you what, Moon," Clint said. "Why don't you tell me whatever you know about those robbers, and when I'm ready to go after them, I'll come and talk to you again."

"Talkin's about all I can do anymore," Cole Moon said sadly.

"I don't know about that," Clint said, "but why don't we wait and see?"

"Well," Moon said, rubbing his lean, gray-stubbled jaw, "I don't know a hell of a lot . . ."

NINE

When Clint returned to the buckboard, Liz was waiting there in an agitated state. He noticed that the back of the wagon was well stocked with supplies. He felt guilty for a moment, but even if he had been there he couldn't have helped her load the wagon.

"Where have you been?" she asked anxiously. "I was worried."

"I'm fine," Clint said. "I was just talking to some people."

"Did you send your telegraph message?"

"Yes."

"Did you see the doctor?"

Clint frowned. He'd forgotten about that.

"You didn't, did you?" she asked.

"No," he said, "but I feel fine—"

"Let's go over there now," she said, cutting him off.

"Liz—"

"You want to argue with me, Clint?"

"Don't say my name so loud, Liz—"

"Then are we going to the doctor's office, or am I gonna shout your name all over town?"

"That's blackmail."

"That's right," she said, setting her jaw firmly.

"All right," he said, "lead the way."

The doctor was surprised to see Clint, but he was obviously pleased. After he examined him he was even more pleased.

"Your progress is better than I would have hoped," he said. "How did you feel during the ride?"

Since Liz wasn't in the examining room with them, Clint told the truth.

"It was hell," Clint said.

"But you did it anyway," the doctor said. "That's good, but don't push it. I wouldn't recommend making this trip again for a while."

"The next time I make this trip, Doc," Clint said, "it'll be on horseback."

"Well," the doctor said, "I'll be out to see you a couple of more times before then. All in all, though, I'd say you were doing nicely—wonderfully, in fact. You can get dressed."

While Clint was dressing, the doctor asked, "Have you been to see the sheriff?"

"You mean the new sheriff? The schoolteacher?"

"Tom's doing the best he can, Clint."

"The man has no experience as a lawman, Doc," Clint said. "He could have the best intentions in the world, but when push come to shove, he's going to get killed."

"What would you suggest?" the man asked. "That we give the job back to Cole Moon?"

"Cole Moon has over forty years of experience with law-keeping, Doc. You could do a damn sight worse. In fact, I think you have."

"That remains to be seen," the doctor said.

"You and this Tom Slater wouldn't be friends, would you?"

"We are."

"I see," Clint said. "Well, I meant no disrespect. I'm sure he was a fine teacher."

The doctor smiled at that and said, "Actually, he was lousy at it. That's why he wanted to switch."

"Well," Clint said, "let's hope he's better at learning than he was at teaching."

Clint started for the door, but stopped short of it.

"Doc, let me ask you something."

"Go ahead."

"When was the last time you examined Cole Moon?"

"I've never examined Cole Moon."

"But you've seen him."

"Well . . . yes, on the street . . ."

"What do you think of him? I mean, his physical condition?"

"Well, when he was sheriff he looked fit and healthy enough for a man his age, but since then he seems to have deteriorated."

"Can you think of a medical reason for that?"

"Only that he might not be taking proper care of himself, eating the way a man his age should. I know he's drinking too much, because I've seen him drunk myself."

"Could there be another reason for his condition?" Clint asked. "I mean, not a medical one?"

"Of course," the doctor said. "There could be several, but are you asking me if his physical condition is a result of his losing his job?"

"I guess that's what I'm asking you."

"I'd have to say that's probably the case," the doctor said. "I mean, I'm sure there's a medical reason for his run-down state, but I think the medical reason could be a result of his losing his job. He has no self-worth at the moment, so he's not taking care of himself."

"So if he did start to take care of himself, his condition might improve."

"I would say so, yes."
Clint nodded and said, "Thanks, Doc."
"See you in a couple of weeks, Mr. Adams."
"Right."

In the waiting room Liz rose as Clint came out.
"What did he say?"
"He said I was fine."
Liz frowned.
"Should I go and talk to him myself?"
"Why would I lie to you, Liz?" he asked. "He said I was progressing better than he would have thought. If you want to hear it from him, then go ahead."

She studied him for a moment, then said, "No, I'll take your word for it. Do you want to rest before we start back?"

"No," he said. "Let's start back now. I'll have plenty of time to rest when we get there."

As they left the doctor's office and walked back to the buckboard, Clint was thinking that he was very satisfied with his trip to town. The next time he was in town, he'd get the rest of the information he needed, and then the hunting would start.

He had never been so anxious to hunt men as he was at that moment.

TEN

The first morning that Clint woke and stretched without thinking first about what it would do to his back, he knew it was time to leave. Liz, watching him, also knew.

"You'll be leaving today, won't you?"

"Yes."

"I wish I had known that last night," she said.

"Why?"

She smiled and said, "We could have made it last longer."

He smiled back and said, "I'll just be going from here to town. I don't have to leave *that* early. We can make it last longer right now."

He lay back down and pulled her to him. Her mouth descended hungrily onto his, and her hand moved between them, groping for him, finding him and holding him tightly.

"If I hang on to you like this," she whispered, "you *can't* leave."

"I could," he said, "but I'd have to leave something behind."

She smiled, and then the smile died. She released her hold on him.

"No," she said, "I'd want all of you or none of you."

"I can give you all of me, Liz," he said, "but just for right now."

She kissed him and said, "I'll take right now and be happy with it."

Liz watched as Clint saddled Duke. A couple of times she wanted to help him, but decided not to offer. Clint was grateful for that, even though a couple of times he was going to *ask* for her help.

Once Duke was saddled, he turned and faced her.

"Will you stop back this way before you . . . leave town?"

"I don't think so, Liz," he said.

"It's probably just as well."

"Liz . . . I can't tell you how I appreciate what you've done for me."

She waved her hands at him and said, "Don't start thankin' me, Clint Adams. You've done a lot for me, too, so I think we're even."

"We're far from even," he said, "but . . ."

She walked him outside, and before he mounted up they embraced for a long time.

"Good-bye," he said.

"Don't get killed," she said, wiping away a tear.

"I'll do my best," he promised.

He rode away having already decided that he wouldn't look back.

When Clint rode into Dogtown again he had a full beard and long hair. Of course, there was nothing he could do to disguise Duke, but he hoped that his appearance would be different enough to keep anyone from readily recognizing him.

He rode to the livery and told the liveryman that he'd be leaving Duke for one night only.

"Pay in advance," the man said, extending his hand. Clint paid him.

He went to the hotel next and took a room, then went to see the doctor. He wanted to tell the man he was in town, and warn him not to blurt out his name on the street if they happened to meet.

"Is there a reason for that?" the doctor asked.

"Yes," Clint said. "People think I'm dead, and I'd like to keep it that way for a while."

"Until you find the men who shot you."

"Yes."

"And then you'll kill them."

"Do you really want me to answer that?"

"No," the doctor said, "I'd rather you didn't. All right, I'll keep quiet."

"Thank you."

"But before you leave," the man said, "I want to examine you."

Clint agreed, and undressed to allow it.

"All right," the doctor said just ten minutes later, "you can get dressed. How'd your back take the ride in?"

"A lot better than the buckboard ride last month."

"But it still pains you, doesn't it?"

"Yes," Clint said, "but it's time to stop lying around and get on with living."

"You've put back some weight, too, I see."

"I feel all right, Doc," Clint said, dressing. "Thanks for everything."

"I wish I could take credit, but I can't," the man said. "The truth is, you just wanted to heal, and you did."

Clint shook the man's hand, paid him what he owed him, and left.

He walked to the end of town to the rooming house and saw Cole Moon sitting on the porch, where he had left him.

THE ROAD TO TESTIMONY

He couldn't see anything different about the man until he mounted the porch and Moon turned his head to look at him. Immediately Clint saw that the man's eyes were clear and sharp, his lips no longer had that bloodless look, and he wasn't as pale as he had been. He still looked thin, grizzled, and old, but he was not the same man Clint had spoken to the month before.

"Well," Moon said, "you took your sweet time comin' back. When do we leave?"

ELEVEN

Clint sat and explained to Cole Moon what had to be done before they could start looking for the four bank robbers, who—hopefully—were the same men who had shot him in the back and left him to die.

"First of all," Clint said, "where would we look after all this time?"

The old man rubbed his jaw and said, "The trail's stone cold."

"That's right," Clint said. "What we need is some information on where they might have gone."

"Where would we get that?"

"The last time we spoke," Clint said, "you told me that one of them worked in the bank as a teller for a while."

"Less than a month. Just long enough to get people to knowin' him and trustin' him." He shook his head. "People trust bank tellers more than they trust the law."

"It has something to do with handing them your money," Clint said. "You have to trust someone to do that."

"So how does that help us?" the old man asked.

"I'm going to talk with some of the employees of the bank

and see what they can tell me about the fella. Do you remember the name he used?"

"Hell, no. I only knew him as the teller at the bank."

"Did you ever give him any of your money, Cole?" Clint asked.

"Be damned if I'll put *my* money into a bank!" the old man said. "I may be old, but I ain't stupid—not yet!"

Clint couldn't believe the change that had come over Cole Moon. The grizzled old lawman told him that he had gotten to thinking about what Clint had said, and knew that he had to get out there and find those bank robbers, or else die sitting on that porch.

"That waren't the way I was meant to die," Moon said. "You and me, we're gonna die the same way, Clint—and *not* from a bullet in the back."

"No," Clint said, "we're too ornery for that, right?"

"Damned right."

He didn't know how long or how far the man would be able to go in the saddle, but he felt a damn sight better chasing four men with Cole Moon at his side, no matter how old he was.

He wondered just *how* old that was.

Clint walked to the bank and entered. All Moon had remembered about the robber who worked in the bank is that he had been a fancy-looking dude. The young women in town had all set their hats for him, Moon said, not that he could see why, and the man did seem to have a way with the ladies.

When Clint saw the lovely young woman sitting at the desk in the bank, he forgot about talking to the other employees. This was the one who would be able to tell him what he wanted to know. Before he could speak to her, though, he was going to have to get a haircut and a beard trim. He didn't want the beard shaved, just trimmed nice and neat. That done, he'd head right for the young lady, whose nameplate said that she was Miss Polly Haskell. After that he'd approach the bank president with the story he'd prepared, and get the man's blessings to speak to the bank employees. Polly Haskell was about twenty-two, clear-skinned, auburn-haired, slender, and sweet-looking, and any man who worked in the bank who had a way with women would not have been able to resist making a try for her.

Hell, Clint was looking forward to it himself.

TWELVE

After Clint had his haircut and beard trim he returned to the bank and stopped in front of Polly Haskell's desk. It took Polly Haskell a few moments to realize he was there, and then when she looked up she was startled.

"Oh," she said, "I'm sorry, I didn't see you . . . at first."

"I didn't mean to startle you," he said in his most charming manner.

"Can I help you?"

"I'd like to see the bank president."

"Mr. Quimby?"

"If that's his name."

"Can I tell him what it's about?" she asked.

"Yes," Clint said, "tell him it's about ten thousand dollars."

"Ten thousand . . . dollars?" she asked. "You want to make a deposit or . . . or take out a loan?"

"Neither," Clint said. "Tell him I want to try to get it back for him."

She was obviously unsure how to respond, so she finally stood up and said, "I'll . . . I'll see if he has time to see you."

"Fine," he said, smiling. "Thank you."

She left her desk and went to a door that presumably led to the president's office. She knocked and then entered, and Clint waited patiently. After a few moments the door opened and Polly Haskell came back out, followed by a florid-faced man in his sixties, who was dressed in a three-piece suit that was banker's gray.

"Excuse me," the man said, "my name is Harold Quimby. How may I help you?"

"I'm afraid you have that backward, Mr. Quimby," Clint said. "I'm here to help you."

"In what way?"

"Didn't this lovely young lady tell you?" Clint asked. He looked at Polly Haskell, who blushed and looked away. "I want to help you get your money back."

"What money would that be?"

"Why, the money that was stolen from this bank three months ago."

Quimby studied Clint for a few moments, then said, "Perhaps we'd better talk in my office."

"Yes, why don't we?" Clint looked at Polly Haskell and said, "Thank you, Miss Haskell. Seeing you has brightened my day."

"Oh, my . . ." Polly Haskell said, and blushed again.

Clint followed Quimby into his office. The bank president closed the door behind them and then went around his desk and sat down.

"Mr. . . ."

"Cullen," Clint said. "My name is Cullen." He had chosen the name because he knew there *wasn't* a bounty hunter operating under that name. Also, it had a strong yet nonthreatening sound to it.

"Uh . . . Mr. Cullen, just what is your business?"

"I'm a bounty hunter, Mr. Quimby," Clint said.

THE ROAD TO TESTIMONY

"I see. Then your interest in this . . . robbery is the price on the head of the men who committed it?"

"That's right," Clint said, "but I figured there might be a reward involved if I found and returned the money that was stolen."

"Mr. Cullen, how much do you know about banks?"

"Not much," Clint said. "You put money in, you take money out."

Quimby laughed condescendingly and said, "Well, there's a little more to it than that. Our bank is insured. You see, the ten thousand dollars that was stolen from us three months ago had already been replaced. No one—not the bank, and not our depositors—has lost a dime."

"Let me understand this, Mr. Quimby," Clint said. "If I find that money, the bank *doesn't* want it back?"

"Well . . . it sounds a little ridiculous when you put it that way, but yes, essentially that's what I'm trying to say."

Clint was surprised, but thought he might still make this work to his advantage.

"Mr. Quimby, would you have any objection to my speaking to some of your employees?"

"About what?"

"Well, I understand that one of the robbers worked for you for about three weeks before the robbery. Is that true?"

"Uh . . ." Quimby fidgeted in his chair uncomfortably. "Uh . . . well, yes, that is true . . ."

"And did you hire him?"

"I, uh, I did, yes."

"Then he made a fool out of you, didn't he, sir?"

Quimby looked the fool and said, "Yes, I suppose he did."

"Wouldn't you like to see him caught and punished?" Clint asked.

"Mr. Cullen," the bank president said, "I would like to see him drawn and quartered."

"Well, if I talk to your employees—and if you let it be known that they can talk to me—I might be able to make that happen."

Quimby stared at Clint and then said, "Mr. Cullen, you will have the full cooperation of my staff."

"Thank you, Mr. Quimby."

"Come with me, sir," Quimby said, rising from his seat and walking purposefully to his door.

They went out into the bank, and Quimby made a quick announcement to his employers—along with some depositors—that they were to cooperate fully with Mr. Cullen.

"Mr. Cullen," Quimby said, "they're all yours."

"Thank you, sir."

"Not at all," Quimby said, "and if there's anything else I can do for you, don't hesitate to call on me."

"I won't."

Quimby went into his office, and all of the bank's employees—all seven of them—stared at Clint expectantly.

"Go on about your work," Clint said. "I'll only want to speak to each of you in turn for a few minutes—all except you, Miss Haskell." He lowered his voice and leaned over Polly Haskell's desk as he spoke.

"Uh, m-me?"

"It is *Miss* Haskell, isn't it?"

"Well . . . yes . . . but . . . I don't know what I could tell you—"

"Perhaps we'll find out," he said, "tonight, over dinner."

"Dinner? I, uh, don't know—"

"Mr. Quimby *did* say that you were to cooperate with me, didn't he?"

"Yes, but—"

"Then I'll pick you up at seven," Clint said. He picked up a piece of paper from her desk and set it down in front of her. "Just tell me where to pick you up."

THE ROAD TO TESTIMONY 51

Polly Haskell, flustered and confused, wrote on the slip of paper and then handed it back to Clint, who read it and put it in his pocket.

"Thank you, Miss Haskell," he said. "I'll see you at seven."

"Yes," Polly Haskell said, "at seven."

As Clint—or "Cullen," as she knew him—walked away, she wondered why she couldn't get her heart to stop pounding.

Clint spent about an hour talking to the other bank employees. Three of them were men, two over thirty-five, and one about twenty. None of them knew much about the man who had worked there for three weeks before robbing the bank, other than that his name was Dick Bonner. Clint knew that the man wouldn't have been stupid enough to use his real name, but he had probably used his real initials.

The other three employees were women, but they were all over fifty, and none of the three of them knew *anything* about Mr. Bonner except that he was a nice young man, quite handsome, very popular with the female depositors, and, oh, yes, he was quite insistent in his pursuance of Miss Haskell.

"He liked her a lot," Miss Emily Todd said.

"And she him?" Clint asked.

Miss Todd—all of sixty-five, and quite feisty, from what Clint could tell—stared at him with her clear blue eyes and said, "Oh, no, she would have nothing to do with him."

"Why not?" Clint asked, "If he was so handsome—"

"Miss Haskell is quite shy," Emily said, "and Mr. Bonner was *so* persistent . . ."

"He frightened her?"

"Oh, yes," the old woman said. "Now, if I was just twenty years younger and he was *half* as insistent—well, I tell you I was quite a catch in my day."

He believed her.

"I'm sure you were, Miss Todd. I'm only sorry we didn't meet then."

"Oh . . ." she said. "You would have enjoyed it, Mr. Cullen, you surely would have."

Clint leaned over and kissed her cheek and said, "I don't doubt it for a minute."

"Mr. Cullen," she called as he walked away.

"Yes?"

"Miss Haskell is very young and inexperienced," she said. "An older man like yourself could do wonders for her."

"Why, Miss Todd, are you playing matchmaker?"

"Oh, heavens, no," Miss Todd said. "You would make *any* woman a *terrible* husband—"

"Why, thank you."

"—but you'd make a *wonderful* adventure for *any* woman," Miss Todd finished.

"Even you, Miss Todd?"

"Especially me, Mr. Cullen."

As Clint left the bank he found himself genuinely disappointed that he *hadn't* met Emily Todd years ago.

THIRTEEN

Clint went back to his hotel at five to get ready for his dinner with Polly Haskell. His intention was to have a bath, and then don some new clothes he had bought that day. When he entered the lobby, however, he found a man waiting for him—a man wearing a badge. As the lawman stood up, Clint deliberately bypassed him—it was what "Cullen" would have done—and went to the desk to arrange for his bath. When he turned around, the sheriff was facing him.

"Is your name Cullen?" the man asked.

"That's right," Clint said. "I assume you're Sheriff Slater?"

"That's right," Slater said. He was tall, dark-haired, and very slender. He wore a gun on his hip that was as out of place as if it were a curved saber. "I'd like to have a word with you."

"Anywhere in particular you want to do this, Sheriff?" Clint asked. "I was planning on having a bath."

"I won't keep you very long," the teacher-turned-lawman said, "and right here is as good a place as any."

"All right, then," Clint said, "talk."

"I understand you're a bounty hunter."

"So?"

"I also understand you've been asking a lot of questions at the bank."

"So?" Clint said, again. "Get to the point, Sheriff. I have a dinner appointment."

"I don't want any trouble here, Mr. Cullen."

"That makes two of us, Sheriff," Clint said, "because I'm not looking for any trouble, either—at least, not here in Dogtown."

"You're after the money?" Slater asked.

"What else would I be after?" Clint said, playing his "Cullen" guise to the hilt.

"If you find that money, I'll expect you to return it to the bank."

"Is that a fact?" Clint said. "Now, why would you expect me to do that when even the bank doesn't expect it?"

"What?"

"Maybe you'd better have a talk with your bank president, Sheriff," Clint said, patting the man on the arm. "Now, if you'll excuse me, I have a bath waiting."

He walked past the confused lawman and went upstairs to get his new clothes. He wanted to change into them right from the bath.

Freshly bathed and newly dressed, Clint stepped out onto the street with almost an hour still to go before he was to pick up Polly Haskell for dinner. He decided to go to the saloon and nurse a beer for that long.

The bartender remembered him, and as he brought him his beer, asked, "How's that back of yours?"

"Stiff," Clint said, "but a helluva lot better than it was, thanks."

"You're all spruced up," the bartender said. "All you need is something sweet-smelling to wear."

"I don't believe in it," Clint said, wrinkling his nose. "I believe a man should smell like a man. I think that's what women want, not some sweet-smelling dandy."

The saloon was busy at this time of the evening, and the bartender excused himself to take some other drink orders, from both customers and the girls who were working the floor.

"Any particular woman in mind?" the bartender asked when he returned.

Clint didn't mind talking with the man. It was a way to pass the time. There were a couple of poker games going on that he wouldn't have minded sitting in on, but he never sat down to play poker unless that was *all* he had on his mind. He hated playing poker with a time limit.

"Little lady from the bank," he replied.

The bartender's eyes widened and he said, "Polly Haskell?"

"Well, I'm not talking about Miss Todd."

"A lot of men in this town are carrying a torch for Polly," the bartender said.

"Present company included."

The man smiled sheepishly and said, "I had a crush on her myself for a while, yeah, but I decided she was too sweet-looking for me. My kind of woman is one of these girls here, Maggie or Nora. Polly Haskell wouldn't know how to handle herself in a place like this."

"You're right, there."

Clint looked around at Kim and Nora. He didn't know which was which, but they were of a type: hard-edged good looks and a watch-your-step attitude that came from years of working in saloons.

"Plannin' on stayin' in town longer this time?" the bartender asked.

"Just overnight," Clint said. "I'll be leaving in the morning."

He waited for the bartender to ask him where he was going, but that would have gone beyond conversation into downright nosy, and the man didn't do it. He knew his job and place too well.

The bartender drifted off then to work hard for the next half hour or so, so Clint just stood at the bar, nursing his beer until the bartender brought a second one on the house. When the clock on the wall said he had ten minutes to go he waved at the bartender, dropped some money on the bar, and left.

FOURTEEN

Polly Haskell's room was above the hardware store, with a side entrance. Clint had to climb a sturdy set of wooden steps, which was as they should be, since they were attached to the side of that store. Still, Polly Haskell didn't seem the type who should be living above a hardware store. He saw her as more the picket-fence type, with a garden and a nice porch. Well, maybe that's where she *would* live when she got married.

He knocked on the door, and when she answered it he barely recognized her. Her brown hair, which had been in a bun at the bank, was now down around her shoulders, and she wasn't wearing the little wire-rim glasses she had been wearing earlier. Even the lines of her face seemed softer this evening. At the bank she had been pretty, but in a cool, efficient way. Tonight she was warm and lovely-looking, and Clint could see where most of the men in town might be sweet on her.

"Is something wrong?" she asked.

"Uh, no, I just, uh, you're not wearing your glasses tonight."

"Oh," she said, putting her hand to her face, as if to adjust the nonexistent glasses. "No, I only need them at work."

"And your hair is lovely."

"Thank you," she said.

"Shall we go?"

"Yes," she said. "I'll just get my wrap."

He waited while she went inside, and reappeared momentarily.

As they walked down the steps he said, "I'll have to leave the choice of a place to eat to you."

"I know a small place."

Clint knew a lot of small places in a lot of towns across the West that served very good food. They were usually run by families, and the cooking was good, down-home cooking. The place where Polly took him was no different. He knew as soon as they walked in and he smelled the aromas in the air that the food was going to be good, and the coffee black and strong.

They both ordered steaks and vegetables, and Clint had a small pot of coffee while they were waiting.

"How did you come to live above the hardware store?" he asked.

"Oh, my father owns it," she said. "He lives behind it, but when I turned nineteen he gave me the two rooms upstairs."

"That was nice of him."

"Not so nice," she said with a smile. "He charges me rent. He says that if I'm earning my own keep, I should pay for my room."

"He sounds—"

"Stubborn," she said. "He's disappointed that I'm not married. I half expect him to keep raising my rent until I *have* to get married."

"He wouldn't do that, would he?"

"Yes, he would."

"Well," he said, making his tone conspiratorial, "from what I understand there are any number of men in this town who would like to help him out."

THE ROAD TO TESTIMONY

She blushed and said, "I am aware that I am the subject of ridicule—"

"Whoa," he said. "Who said anything about ridicule?"

"What would you call it?"

"My understanding is that there are men in this town who are . . . kind of sweet on you."

"They smile when I walk by, and then they talk behind my back," she said. "None of them has the nerve to . . . to even do what you've done."

"What have I done?"

"You don't even know me and you invited me to dinner," she said.

"No one's ever asked you to dinner?"

"I have had other kinds of offers," she said with a stern look, "but no, no one has."

"I find that hard to believe."

"The men in this town are . . ." she started, and then just trailed off. "We're not here to talk about this. What is it you wanted to ask me about the bank robbery?"

"Well . . . specifically I wanted to ask about this man Dick Bonner. What do you know about him?"

"Nothing."

"I understood that he . . . might have made some advances toward you."

"He did."

"And?"

"I rebuffed him."

"Why?"

"He was crude. Oh, he was polite to everyone else, and he was very pleasant-looking, but he seemed intent on being as crude as he possibly could when it came to me."

"In what way?"

"Suggestive remarks when he knew that no one else was listening." She was apparently very disapproving when it came to that sort of thing, probably the result of a very strict upbringing.

"So then you didn't spend any significant amount of time talking to him?"

"No," she said. "I spent as little time as I could talking to him."

"I see," Clint said, frowning.

Dinner came, and they fell to eating. Clint was rather disappointed. He had hoped that Polly could give him some kind of lead as to where to start looking for "Dick Bonner." Obviously she couldn't, and neither had anyone else in the bank. He was staring at a cold trail, and the coldness seemed to be creeping into the pit of his stomach.

Was it possible that he *wasn't* going to be able to find these men after all?

FIFTEEN

Since Polly Haskell *couldn't* help him, Clint quickly decided not to spend any more time on the subject, and started her talking about herself again. Although reluctant, once she got started, she seemed quite willing to talk about her childhood, her disappointing adult life in Dogtown, and what plans she had for her life.

"I want to go to San Francisco and work in a bank," she said. "Mr. Quimby has told me that he knows people in banking there and that he can get me a job."

"How long has he been telling you that?" Clint asked.

"Oh, quite some time."

"And he hasn't done anything about it yet?"

"Well . . . he keeps inviting me into his office to talk about it, or to dinner—"

"Polly—" Clint started, but she cut him off quickly.

"Oh, Mr. Cullen—"

"Just call me Cl——uh, Cully," he said. He had almost told her to call him "Clint."

"Cully," she said, "I am not a foolish young girl. I know what Mr. Quimby wants . . . but . . ."

"But what?"

She firmed her jaw and said, "But if I truly intend to get out of Dogtown and go to San Francisco, then maybe I'll just have to—"

"Never mind," he said, waving his hand. "Tell Mr. Quimby to go twist in the wind."

"I beg your pardon?"

"I know some people in San Francisco, Polly," he said. "I can probably get you a job. It might not be in banking, but you can take care of that later. Your immediate goal is to *get* to San Francisco, right?"

"That's right."

"Then if I got you a job in, say, a hotel, you'd take it?"

"Well . . . yes . . . but—"

"All right, then," Cullen said. "I'll have to send a few telegrams tomorrow before I leave town. Polly, you'll have to have some faith in me and believe that once I leave town I won't forget all about it. Sometime in the future you'll be getting a telegram from me, or from someone in San Francisco, about this. You'll just have to take that on faith."

She studied him for a few moments and then said, "I do believe you, Cully, but . . ."

"But what?"

". . . why?"

"Why what?"

"Why would you help me like this?" she asked. "You don't even know me."

"Sure I do," he said. "I think I probably know you better than any man in this town does . . . with the possible exception of your father."

"No," she said, shaking her head, "no exception. You know me better than my father does. I find you . . . an amazing man, Cully."

"Well, don't," he said. "I'm just a man like any other man—"

"Not so," she said. "You're not anything like the men in this town. I've been offered other jobs here, Cully, but they always depend on my . . . cooperation, if you know what I mean."

"Yes," he said, "I'm afraid I do know what you mean. Polly, I'd never force a woman to do something she didn't want to do."

"Do you see what I mean?" she said eagerly. Her face was very animated, and had transformed from being lovely to beautiful. "That's the very statement that makes you so unusual and amazing."

"I think I had better take you back home," he said.

She sat back in her chair abruptly, as if he had slapped her.

"All right," she said meekly.

He walked her back to her room, and stopped at the bottom of the stairs.

"I'm sorry I couldn't help you more with information on the robbery," she said.

"Did you see the other men? Were you there?"

"Yes, I was there," she said. "The other men had masks on their faces, covering the lower portion of their face. Bonner was the only one without a mask."

"How did the robbery happen?"

"Bonner produced a gun from behind his teller cage, and then the other two men came in."

"Two men?"

"Yes. There was a third, but he was holding the horses outside."

"I see."

"They robbed the bank, scared everyone, and left."

"That's it?"

"That's all."

"All right," he said, "thanks for spending the time with me, Polly."

"I should be thanking you—"

"You can thank me if and when I *do* get you a job in San Francisco, but rest assured, I'll try."

"I know you will."

"Well . . . good night, then."

She hesitated, then said, "Yes, good night."

"I'll be leaving early in the morning, so . . ."

"Good-bye, then."

"Good-bye."

"And good luck."

He watched her go up the stairs and through her doorway, then turned and headed for the hotel.

SIXTEEN

When he got to the hotel, there was a dark figure on the porch. He might have put his hand on his gun if he hadn't recognized the figure, even in silhouette. It was difficult not to. Cole Moon was a hard man *not* to recognize.

Moon had been seated, but was standing as Clint reached him.

"So?" Moon asked. "What did we find out?"

"Not much," Clint said glumly.

He told Moon everything he had learned from the people in the bank—which was nothing.

"Well," Moon said, rubbing his jaw, "seems I been gettin' all worked up for nothin', huh?"

"Ah, it's my fault, Cole," Clint said. "I want these men so bad I just *knew* I'd come up with *something*. I wouldn't even allow myself to think that I might not."

"What are you gonna do now?"

"I don't know," Clint said. "I'll have to think it over tonight and make a decision in the morning."

"Well," Moon said, "I'll be on my porch in the morning. You let me know what you decide."

Clint watched the old man walk away and was saddened by the fact that when he left in the morning Cole Moon might go back to being that old, *old* man he had first met on the porch of the rooming house.

He had to come up with *some* way to pick a direction in which to go.

He was in his room and had removed his new clothes when there was a knock on the door. He pulled on his pants again and went to the door. He was surprised when he opened it to find Polly Haskell standing in the hall.

"Polly."

"I remembered something," she said eagerly. She slid past him without waiting for an invitation, and he closed the door.

"What did you remember?"

"Something that Bonner said in the bank before he and his friends left."

"What was that?"

"He invited me to go with him," she said. "He said I'd enjoy life in Testimony."

"Life in Testimony?" Clint repeated.

"That's what he said."

"What did he mean by that?"

"I don't know," she said helplessly. "I was just excited about having remembered it, and wanted to come right over and tell you."

"Well, I appreciate it, Polly," Clint said.

"Can you figure out what it means?"

"Well," Clint said, "I doubt that Bonner is very religious, so I suspect that the Testimony he's talking about must be a place."

"A town?"

"If it is, it's one I never heard of," Clint said, "but then I never heard of Dogtown before I came here."

THE ROAD TO TESTIMONY 67

"Well," she said, "*I'd* much rather live in a place called Testimony than a place called Dogtown."

She walked to the window, which overlooked the main street, and gazed out. He walked up behind her and stood there, not touching her.

"I lied," she said.

"About what?"

"About why I came over here."

"What kind of lie?"

She craned her neck to look up at him without turning.

"I did remember what Bonner had said, but I also wanted to come to . . . to . . ."

"To what, Polly?"

She turned to face him and said, "You know what I'm trying to say . . . or are you just not interested? You've probably had so many women in your life that you're just not interested in someone like—"

He silenced her by putting his finger against her lips. Then he removed it, leaned over and kissed her, gently at first, then with more fervor as *her* ardor grew. Soon she was clinging to him desperately, and he turned and maneuvered her over to the bed.

"Is this really what you want?" he asked.

"Yes, oh, yes," she whispered.

He undressed her slowly, unwrapping her like a present, and finally she started to whisper impatiently, "Oh, hurry, do hurry . . ."

When her breasts were bare he kissed them and she gasped. Then he held them—they were like peaches in his hands—and sucked them, and a tremor ran through her. Finally he lowered her to the bed and undressed himself. As he climbed into bed with her she reached for him anxiously, and he entered her cleanly and smoothly. She was inexperienced, but she wasn't a virgin.

Her body was remarkably responsive to the touch of his body, his hands, his mouth as again and again she reached heights she had not reached as many times in her entire young life.

"My God," she said later, lying in his arms.
"Are you all right?"
"I'm . . . marvelous," she said. "I don't think I've ever been happier."
"Polly—" Clint said, but she cut him off, knowing what he was getting at.
"Oh, don't worry, Cully," she said. "I'm not about to ask you to take me with you. I'm inexperienced with men, but I'm not that foolish. I just want you to know how happy you've made me tonight."
"I'm glad."
"You've also shown me that all men aren't a waste of time," she said. "I was starting to doubt that any man could show me that."
"There are plenty of men who won't be a waste of time, Polly," he said, "and you'll meet them."
"I won't meet them in Dogtown," she said. "Maybe I'll meet them in San Francisco."
"I don't know where you'll meet them," Clint said, "but one of them will be the right man for you."
"Do you think I'm worried about being an old maid?" she asked. "That's my father's worry. I don't mind getting old, and I don't even mind if I'm alone. I just don't want to grow old without ever having seen or done anything."
"I can't fault you for that," Clint said. "I'm sure a lot of young men and women feel the same."
"What about you?" she asked. "Have you done everything you ever wanted to do?"
He thought a moment, then said, "Pretty much. In fact, I've

done a lot of things I never wanted to do."

"That sounds . . . sad."

"Not sad," Clint said, "I'm not sad."

He shifted on the bed, trying to get comfortable because his back was hurting.

"I'd better go," she said.

"You don't have to."

She leaned over and kissed him warmly.

"Not for you or me, but for my father," she said. "I don't want to have to explain anything to him in the morning."

She got out of bed and dressed while he watched with enjoyment. She came to the bed again and kissed him, longer this time, using her tongue and moaning as she withdrew.

"Oh, I don't want to go," she said. "I won't ever see you again."

"Polly—"

"I know," she said, touching his face. "I know. I'll wait to hear from you, or from San Francisco. I know you'll do the best you can for me, Cully."

She walked to the door and he almost called out to her, to tell her that his name wasn't Cully, but Clint Adams, but in the end he kept silent and let her go.

Maybe, someday, he'd see her in San Francisco.

SEVENTEEN

Clint found Cole Moon on the porch of the rooming house the next morning, as promised.

"Testimony," he said.

"What kind?" Moon asked.

"It's the name of a place, I think," Clint said. "Does it ring any bells with you?"

"Testimony," Moon said to himself, shaking his head, "Testimony . . ."

"Well," Clint said, "it's the only lead we have, so we'll have to follow it up. Are you ready to do some riding?"

"I'm ready."

"Are you up to it?"

The old man laughed and said, "We're gonna find that out, ain't we?"

Clint moved his shoulders, trying to loosen his back, which was tight this morning, and said, "I guess the same goes for both of us."

EIGHTEEN

They left town that morning and rode in the direction the robbers must have taken. By noon they had reached the gully where Clint had been bushwhacked, and they camped right there.

"Seems to me you wouldn't want to be anywheres near this place," Cole Moon said over coffee.

"You've got that wrong, Cole," Clint said. "This is exactly where I want to be."

Moon knew what Clint meant. This was where he had almost bought it, and he wanted to start his search for the men who had done it from here.

"Which way you figure they went from here?" Clint asked.

Moon looked up, looked around them, and said, "I'd go south."

"Why?" Clint asked. "I mean, aside from your experience telling you to go that way."

"If we just robbed a bank," Moon said, "going west or north wouldn't get us far enough away from Dogtown."

"And east?"

"I just don't see this job bein' pulled by Easterners," Moon said.

"Why Easterners? They could just be from Nebraska, Kansas—"

"Still not far enough," Moon said. "My guess would be that this Testimony is in New Mexico, or Texas."

Clint said, "I've been thinking the same thing. The next town we come to I'll use the telegraph and check on it. If it's in Texas, I can find out pretty quickly."

"And New Mexico?"

"That'll take a little longer."

"And what if it's not in either one?"

"We'll find it."

"And if it's not a place?"

Clint looked across the fire at Moon and said, "We'll deal with that when the time comes."

Moon decided not to push the point and concentrated on his coffee. Clint picked up the pot and poured himself another cup. If Testimony *wasn't* a place, he didn't know *what* he would do, but it *had* to be a place. What the hell else could it be?

When they reached the next town, he'd telegraph Rick Hartman in Labyrinth. Rick knew the name of every town or settlement in Texas, and would have the answer right on the tip of his tongue.

Clint hoped.

They camped for the night without reaching another town, so sending the message would have to wait until the next morning.

"Next town is likely Palmeiro," Moon said. "Can't think of another one between Dogtown and Palmeiro."

"I've been meaning to ask you this," Clint said.

"Ask what?"

"How did you end up the sheriff in a town called Dogtown?"

Moon laughed.

"There ain't too many jobs for an old lawman like me, you know," he said. "A place called Dogtown was all I could get, and then *they* up and fired me. What's left now?"

"Well," Clint said, "you could always become a bounty hunter."

He was kidding, but Moon took the suggestion seriously.

"I hate bounty hunters," Moon said with feeling. "Most of them ain't worth spit."

Clint declined to comment. He had some friends—some *female* friends, in fact—who were bounty hunters, so he didn't feel the urge to comment.

"You know how many years I been wearin' a badge?" Moon asked.

"Forty years?"

"Forty?" Moon said. "Try fifty. Fifty years of walkin' behind a star. Shit, it's all I know. If I can't do that, I'll just be sittin' on some porch someplace."

"Or out here riding with me," Clint said.

"Ridin' with you was an excuse to get up off that porch and leave Dogtown. There's other towns that'll appreciate my experience."

"I'm sure there are."

"Even if I have to take a job as a deputy, I can give somebody the benefit of my experience, right?"

"That's right."

Moon squinted at Clint and said, "Are you yessin' me, son?"

"Nope," Clint said. "I'm agreeing with you."

"Oh."

When it was time to turn in, they decided to do so without setting a watch. There wasn't any reason for it, and Clint didn't honestly know if either of them had the energy to sit up and keep watch. His back was aching, and all he wanted to do was lie down. He suspected that at sixty-eight, Cole Moon felt about the same. At least he hoped he did. He'd hate to have Moon turn out to be in better condition than he was.

Nah. He didn't think so. In the morning he'd probably have to beg the old man to get up—and then he'd have to *help* him up.

Clint drifted off to sleep without knowing whether Moon was asleep yet.

NINETEEN

Clint woke the next morning to the smell of bacon and coffee. When he opened his eyes the first thing he saw was Cole Moon, crouched over him, holding a cup of coffee out to him.

"Time to get up, young fella," Moon said.

Clint sat up and grimaced at the pain in his back. Thankfully, the pain was fleeting, but it left behind a dull ache. He took the cup and made a thank-you gesture with it.

"What time did you get up?" he asked after he had sipped the coffee. It was the blackest, strongest coffee he'd ever tasted.

"Before first light," Moon said, moving back to the fire to pour himself a cup of coffee. "I hope this is not too strong for you."

Clint sipped again and then said, "No such thing as coffee that's too strong."

"I feel the same way," Moon said. "You'll find out some things about me now that we're riding together, Clint."

"Like what?" Clint said, moving his torso right and left slowly, testing himself before trying to get to his feet. "You rise early, and you drink strong coffee?"

"I *only* drink coffee when I'm on the hunt," Moon said, "and I ain't been on the hunt—a *real* manhunt—in years. And yeah, I get up early, and the longer we go, the stronger I'm gonna get."

"Cole," Clint said, "this isn't the old days—"

"You mind what I say, boy," Moon said. "The longer we go, the stronger I'm gonna get. You'll see."

"Well," Clint said, putting his cup down, "I'll try to keep up."

He braced both hands on the ground, preparatory to trying to get up, but before he could move, Moon stood up, stepped toward him, and extended a hand. Clint looked at the hand, recalling his thoughts of the night before, then shrugged and took it. Moon pulled him to his feet.

"Thanks."

"Yer welcome, young fella," Moon said with a grin.

"Don't keep calling me that, Moon," Clint said.

"Why not?" Moon asked. "I'm twenty-five years older than you. That should give me the right to call you whatever I want."

"Not unless you want to get knocked on your twenty-five-year-older ass it doesn't," Clint said.

Moon put up his hands and said, "Okay, okay, don't get violent on me. I'm just an old geezer, remember."

"Old geezer," Clint said, half to himself, "how about letting me have some of that bacon?"

"Sure thing, young—uh, sure thing," Moon said.

After breakfast they broke camp, and each saddled his own horse. Clint hoped he'd be able to do it without asking for Moon's help, and was satisfied when he did it. He hoped it would get easier as they went along, though.

"That back's really botherin' you, huh?" Moon asked.

THE ROAD TO TESTIMONY

Clint looked at Moon and thought about lying, then thought, what the hell for?

"Yeah," he said, "it's bothering me."

"Yer pushin' yerself."

"I know," Clint said, swinging up into the saddle with a wince.

Moon stared at him for a moment, then swung up into the saddle, almost nimbly. Clint was starting to believe that what Moon said was true. The older geezer *was* going to get stronger as they went along.

Jesus . . . he only hoped he could keep up with the old man.

TWENTY

In the town of Testimony, Texas, Bill Wheaton and Del Beman were sitting across from each other in the Lucky Lady Saloon. They were bored.

"We got to get out of this town for a while," Del Beman said.

"You got somethin' in mind?" Wheat asked.

"I might," Del said. "We could go up north and hit us another bank. My share from that last job is almost gone."

The "last job" he was talking about had not been the Dogtown job. They had robbed two other banks since then. On one job Wheat had gone in and worked as a teller for a while before they pulled the job, and on another they had simply ridden in and done it the old-fashioned way. They had pulled one job in California and one in Arkansas. After both jobs they had hightailed it back to Testimony. On both jobs they'd had the help of both Rich House and Dick Wheeler.

Both House and Wheeler were working in jobs now, while Beman and Wheat simply spent their days in the saloon, or in the whorehouse later in the afternoons. Beman's father—who owned the general store *and* was mayor of Testimony—didn't like his son's way of life. He didn't know about the bank jobs; all he knew was that, since his son stopped working at the store, he hadn't done a decent day's work in his life. He also had no use for Bill Wheaton, whom he felt was a bad influence of his son. Wheaton's father had been a decent, hardworking farmer, but since his father's death, Bill Wheaton had let the farm go to seed—badly.

"You know what bothers the hell out of me?" Wheaton said.

"What?"

"We killed the Gunsmith, and we ain't told no one about it."

Beman sat forward and said with a hiss, "Shut up about that!" and looked around them to see if anyone had heard. "We agreed we weren't gonna talk about that."

"I know, but even though we planted the story in some newspaper, I wish we coulda took credit for it. We'd be big men right now, Del."

"We'd be in jail, you fool!" Beman said. "If anyone finds his body and sees that he was shot in the back . . . we shoulda buried him, that's what we shoulda done."

"You'd a thought somebody woulda found him by now, wouldn't ya?" Wheat asked, disappointed.

"I don't know why I ever let you talk me into goin' after him," Beman said. "From now on we're gonna stick to bank jobs, and we ain't gonna kill anybody less'n they get in our way."

"Listen to you," Wheat said in a hard tone. "Who made you boss all of a sudden?"

"I'm just sayin' I ain't lettin' you stampede me into any more fool moves," Beman said. "Dick and Rich wanna follow you, that's up to them."

"Dick follows me," Wheat said, "and House follows you, you know that."

Beman sat back and said, "I don't know why we bother with either one of them."

"They have their uses," Wheat said.

"Yeah," Beman said, "wavin' guns or holdin' the horses. You and me do all the work."

"That's why you and me take most of the profits," Wheat said. "Don't forget that."

"Speakin' of which," Beman said, "this bank I'm thinkin' about is in Missouri . . ."

Wheat looked thoughtful and said, "We ain't never pulled a job that close to home. You know, it might just be fun."

"You know, Wheat," Beman said, "that's what wrong with you."

"What?"

"You think this shit is fun."

"And it ain't?"

"Hell," Beman said, "it's just somethin' to do."

TWENTY-ONE

As Moon had predicted, the next town they came to *was,* in fact, Palmeiro, Wyoming. Palmeiro was somewhat larger than Dogtown but was generally the same type of town. It had peaked at a certain size, and would grow no larger because there was no good reason for there to be an influx of new blood.

Palmeiro did have a telegraph office, though, and a saloon, of which Clint and Moon were to make good use.

"First the saloon," Clint said. "You cut the dust, then I'll send the telegram."

"Sounds good to me," Moon said.

"I don't think we should spend the night, though," Clint added.

Moon looked at Clint and said, "Your back could probably use a night in a real bed."

Clint scowled at Moon and said, "Stop playing mother hen, Moon. My back is fine."

"Fine," Moon said. "I won't say another damn word about it."

"Good."

"Fine."

"Fine with me."

They had already gone through the same routine many times since leaving Dogtown. Moon seemed to have taken it upon himself to look after Clint's health, which annoyed Clint no end. If anything, *he* should have been looking after the older man, except that—true to his word—Cole Moon *did* seem to be getting stronger as they went along.

Damn his hide.

They rode to the saloon and dismounted. It was near midday, and as they entered there were few enough men in the place that their entry attracted attention. Clint knew that his beard had gone scraggly, and Moon's face was sporting a growth of gray whiskers. They were dirty, and they probably smelled.

They walked to the bar and ordered a beer each, ignoring the looks, until Moon decided to speak.

"You'd think nobody had ever seen a couple of trail bums before," he said, loud enough for everyone in the place to hear.

"You smell somethin', Vern?" a voice from the back asked.

"Hey, old-timer," another man called. He was the man sitting with "Vern."

"Easy," Clint said.

"You talkin' to me?" Moon asked, turning around.

"Yeah, you," the man said. "We don't mind trail bums in our town, as long as they leave the dust out on the trail, where it belongs."

"Yeah," Vern said, "and the smell."

Clint watched the two men in the mirror. They wore trail clothes themselves but looked like ranch hands. Seated the way they were, he couldn't see whether they wore their guns on the right or the left. The right was a good assumption, but there was always that odd left-hander that Fate threw in to see how you handled it.

Moon stared at the two men and then removed his hat and slowly began to pat himself down with it, raising great clouds of dust.

"Hey!" the bartender shouted.

"That enough dust fer you young fellers?" Moon asked.

The two men seemed to take Moon's actions as a personal affront, and they both stood up. Clint was able to see that they both wore their guns on their right hips. Vern stood about six feet tall, with too much gut for a man in his twenties. His partner was slender and stood about five-foot-eight. He looked to be in his early thirties.

"Somebody ought to teach your daddy some manners, friend," Vern called to Clint.

Now, Clint had nothing against the two men, and he wished that Moon hadn't suddenly taken it on himself to turn ornery, but he also knew that since he walked in with Moon, he had to back him.

He turned and said, "You talking to me?"

"Yeah," Vern said, "teach your old man some manners."

"Before *we* do," the other man said.

Clint turned his back and said, "He ain't my old man. If you want him to learn some manners, teach them to him yourselves . . . but be ready to get carried out of here."

"Huh," Vern said. "Who're you kiddin'? This old man ain't no danger to anyone but himself."

"So then what are you bothering with him for?" Clint asked, leaning over his beer mug. "Ignore him and maybe he'll go away."

Everything would have been all right if Moon had kept his mouth shut. The two men were exchanging glances, like they were trying to decide whether to take Clint's advice, when Moon spoke up.

"Come on, ya two jaspers," he said. "Whataya, afraid of an old man?"

"You better watch your mouth, old man," Vern said, pointing at Moon.

"Make me."

"Moon . . ." Clint said.

"That's it," Vern said, crossing the room to Moon. His partner followed behind him.

Moon cackled, something that sounded like "Hee-hee," and swung at Vern. His punch caught the man flush on the jaw. It stopped him, but it surprised him more than it hurt him.

"What the hell—" Vern said, and swung at Moon.

Clint turned quickly and hooked the man's forarm with his own, stopping the punch before it could reach its mark.

"Take it easy," Clint said. "He's just an old man."

"I thought you said he wasn't your old man," the other man said.

"He's not," Clint said, "but he's riding with me. I think all that time on the trail has addled his brain."

"Turn loose of my arm, mister," Vern said, his tone menacing.

"This has gone far enough—" Clint started to say, but before he could finish, Moon took a step and hit Vern in the face again. This time the man was off-balance, and as he started to fall, Clint turned his arm loose so he wouldn't go to the floor with him.

"Damn it!" Vern's partner said, and went for his gun.

"Hold it!" Clint said. He reached forward and pinned the man's hand to his gun so he couldn't clear leather. "There's no call for gunplay."

"You're right," the man said, and he punched Clint with his other hand.

Clint's head rocked back, and he tasted blood from a split lip.

"Shit," he said. He released the man's gun hand and hit him in the face. His blow was harder than the other man's was, and the man staggered back into a table where two other men were playing two-handed poker. The table tipped over, and money went flying.

"Goddammit!" one of the poker players said. Angrily, he lifted the fallen man up and held him while his partner hit him.

"Hey!" Vern said from the floor. He came up and ran to help his friend, and before long the four men were standing and trading blows.

"Hee-hee," Moon cackled again, and moved to join the fray.

"Oh, no," Clint said, grabbing the man's arm. "Let's get out of here."

"Whatsamatter?" Moon asked. "You afraid of a bar fight?"

"I don't want your brittle bones being broken," Clint said, and he dragged Moon from the saloon until they were outside. From within they could hear the sound of men grunting, blows being exchanged, and wood breaking.

"Hey!" someone shouted. It sounded like the bartender.

"Let's get away from here before the law shows up," Clint said.

"Missin' a good fight," Moon said glumly.

"Get your horse and let's move!" Clint said.

As they walked away, leading their horses, Clint asked, "What the hell got into you, anyway?"

"That's the way I used to shake off the trail dust in the old days," Moon explained. "I wanted to see if it still worked."

"And did it?"

"It sure as hell did!"

TWENTY-TWO

They found the telegraph office, and Clint sent off a telegram to Rick Hartman. He requested whatever information Rick had on a place called Testimony, and he signed the telegram "Wild Bill."

"Wild Bill?" Moon asked as they stepped outside.

"Rick knows that Hickok and I were friends."

"Is that a fact?" Moon asked. "I knew Hickok. I mean, I wouldn't say we was friends or nothin', but I knew him pretty well."

"That doesn't surprise me," Clint said.

"It don't?"

"Nah," Clint said. "All you legends probably knew each other."

Moon narrowed his eyes and said, "You makin' fun of me, young'n?"

There were two chairs on the boardwalk outside the telegraph office, so Clint said, "Let's sit here and wait for the answer."

"You think it's gonna come that quick?"

"I don't know," Clint said, "but what would you suggest—

that we go to the saloon and have a drink while we're waiting?"

"Well," Moon said, "there might be a second saloon in town."

"Why?" Clint said, sitting down. "You want to get another one wrecked?"

"That wasn't my fault," Moon said, settling into the chair next to Clint.

"It wasn't?"

"No," Moon said, "it was yours."

"Mine?" Clint asked incredulously. "How do you figure that?"

"You're the one made that feller fall on that table, and that started that whole thing."

"*That* started the whole thing?"

"Sure it did. Before that, everythin' was just fine."

Clint stared at the old man, shaking his head, and then said, "You know, I'm having second thoughts about bringing you along."

Moon smiled, revealing that whatever teeth he had left had gone yellow, and said, "Too late now."

"You know, we'll be lucky to get out of this town without getting thrown in jail."

"Why?" Moon asked, looking innocent. "All we're doin' is settin' here."

"Yeah," Clint said, "*now* we're sitting here."

At that point the telegraph clerk came out of his office and stopped short when he saw them.

"Oh, there you are," the man said. "Thought I was gonna have to go looking for you. Your answer came through, already."

He handed Clint the reply.

"Thanks very much," Clint said.

"You coulda asked me that question, you know," the clerk said. "I knew that."

Clint gave the man a wan smile and said, "Next time."

The man went back inside, and Clint read the reply.

"What's it say?"

"You ever hear of a town called Flatrock?" Clint asked.

"Seems to me I have," Moon said. "Somewhere in Texas, ain't it? Not quite in the panhandle, but real close by."

"Well," Clint said, looking at Moon, "seems it isn't called Flatrock anymore."

"No? What's it called?"

Clint handed Moon the message and said, "It's now called Testimony, and has been for the past ten years or so."

Moon took the telegraph message, read it, and said, "Whataya know about that?"

"You know where Flatrock was?" Clint asked.

Moon looked at Clint and said, "I believe I could find it."

"Then what are we waiting for?" Clint asked, getting up. "Let's get out of here before the sheriff finds us and locks us up for wrecking a saloon."

Moon got up and hurried after Clint, saying, "I tole you that waren't *my* fault, it was *yours*."

"I don't want to talk about it...."

TWENTY-THREE

Clint Adams and Cole Moon stared at the town of Testimony, which had once been called Flatrock.

"Tole you I could find it," Moon said with a smug look on his face.

Clint decided not to point out that they had been going in circles for hours and had probably found the town by accident—if, indeed, they were looking off into the distance at Testimony.

"We don't know for sure that *that* is Testimony," he did say.

"Trust me," Moon said, "it is."

The old man continued to surprise Clint over and over again. Instead of wearing down—the way he himself was—the old man seemed to thrive on the trail. He even *looked* better. His complexion was better, and he didn't look as frail as he once had, although Clint would swear that the man had not put on any weight at all.

More and more he wondered why Moon hadn't gone after the bank robbers himself as soon as the robbery happened. He figured it might be a sore point with the old man, though, so he didn't bring it up.

"We ain't gonna find out if it's Testimony by sitting here, are we?" Moon said suddenly.

"No, we're not."

"By the way."

"What?"

"How's your back, sonny?"

Moon kicked his horse in the ribs and shot forward before Clint could answer.

"My back is fine!" Clint shouted at the man's back, and started after him.

Just outside of town they came to a sign that said: YOU ARE NOW ENTERING TESTIMONY.

"No population," Moon said.

Clint looked straight ahead and said, "Whatever it is, it will soon decrease by four."

"Are they gonna recognize you?" Moon asked.

Clint looked at Moon and said, "I doubt it. Everything happened so fast."

"They must have recognized you *before* they bushwhacked you. That means they know what you look like."

"They know what I looked like before I grew all this hair," Clint said. His beard had become a wild thing on his face, and his hair was almost down to his shoulders. "They're not going to know who I am, but what about you?"

"What *about* me?"

"Did they see you in Dogtown?"

"Hell, no," Moon said. "By the time I got to the bank, they was gone."

"What about the one who called himself Bonner?" Clint asked. "He was in town for a few weeks. Ever talk to him?"

"Let me think," Moon said. "Passed him in the street once or twice, but I don't recollect that we ever had a real conversation."

"Well, you don't exactly look like you did when we left Dogtown," Clint said. "Just keep the beard and we might be safe."

"How many of them will you recognize?" Moon asked.

"Three," Clint said. "The only one I didn't see is the one who backshot me—but I'll be seeing him real soon."

"What if they ain't here?" Moon asked.

Clint hesitated, then said, "I don't know. Let's ride in and find out."

They rode past the signpost and onto the road leading into Testimony, each looking for his own kind of redemption.

Some of the buildings were newer than others, leading Clint to believe that when the town had changed its name it had changed its appearance as well. There were even some buildings that were under construction still, which meant that the town was still growing. Clint wondered what it was about the town, or the area, that was drawing people to Testimony.

They rode to the livery and gave up their horses to the liveryman. They paid for a day and said that they'd pay as they went along, because they didn't know how long they'd be in town.

They took their saddlebags and rifles and from the livery they walked to the hotel. As they entered, the desk clerk looked up at them and frowned.

"We need two rooms," Clint said.

"Yes, sir," the clerk said, sniffing the air, "and baths?"

"What does that—" Moon started, but Clint put his hand on his arm to silence him.

"Not this time, partner," he said, deliberately *not* using Moon's name. He looked at the clerk and said, "Yes, and baths."

"We have those facilities right here, sir," the clerk said proudly. "We also have a barber—"

"Don't press your luck, friend," Clint said, and the clerk fell silent. Moon continued to glare at the young man.

Clint signed in for both of them, and the clerk handed them their keys.

"Do you have any luggage?" the clerk asked.

"No," Clint said, "just our saddlebags." He patted his, which was draped over his shoulder.

"Do you gents know how long you'll be staying?" he asked.

"No," Clint said. "We'll just pay day by day, if that's all right with you."

"Oh, yes, sir, that's just fine," the clerk said. "I'll have your baths drawn immediately. Hot water for both of you?"

"Jesus, no," Moon said, looking aghast. "It's bad enough I got to take a bath, why would I want to take a *hot* one?"

"It, uh, cuts through the grime . . . sir," the clerk said.

"You little—"

"Make mine hot," Clint said, cutting Moon off, "and my friend's cold. All right?"

"Yes, sir," the clerk said. He looked at the register and said, "Hot for Mr. . . . Cullen and cold for Mr. . . . Custer?"

"Custer?" Moon said, looking at Clint quizzically.

"Custer," Clint said, nodding. He looked at the clerk and said, "Thank you. We'll be down shortly."

As they walked up the stairs Moon said to Clint in a low voice, "You know, I *knew* Custer. I mean, I wouldn't say we was friends or anything, but I knew him. . . ."

TWENTY-FOUR

Freshly bathed and having changed their clothes, Clint and Moon stepped outside the hotel.

"You should have let me teach that little shit of a clerk a lesson," Moon said. "Imagine turnin' up his nose at us."

"Why not?" Clint said. "We stunk, didn't we?"

"We smelled the way men are supposed to smell," Moon said, pounding his chest with his fist.

"Tell that to the women in this town who might have run away from us, the way we smelled."

"Women," Moon said, as if Clint had just reminded him of something. "Do you know how long it's been since I had a woman?"

"Twenty years?" Clint said.

Moon gave him a dirty look.

"It was just a guess."

"I'll have you know I was keeping two women in Dogtown real happy while I was sheriff."

Clint thought of a reply immediately, and decided not to use it.

"Really?"

"And they wasn't both as old as me, if that's what yer thinkin'," Moon said. "One was in her fifties, and the other one was in her forties."

"Spring chickens," Clint said.

"Never mind," Moon said. "You and me can make a bet if you want."

"What kind of bet?"

"Let's go and find the whorehouse. We'll each get ourselves a whore, and see who can make his whore howl the loudest."

"That's a bet I think I'll pass on," Clint said. "We've got other things to do."

"How do you want to go about this?" Moon asked, growing serious.

"Well, I guess you can work one side of the street and I'll work the other. Check the stores, the restaurants, saloons, shops, whatever. We'll meet back here and compare notes."

"I got to take notes?" Moon asked. "I don't write so good, you know."

"I just meant we'll meet here and . . . tell each other what we saw."

"And what is it I'm looking for?" Moon asked.

"Oh, that's right," Clint said. "Other than Bonner, you haven't seen any of these men." Clint took a moment to compose his thoughts and then described the three men he had seen as best he could.

"All right," Moon said, nodding his approval, "at least now I know what, or who, I'm lookin' for."

"Now describe Bonner for me."

Moon took a moment to form his thoughts and then said, "A young fella."

Clint waited, and when no more was forthcoming he said, "And?"

"That's all I remember."

"Come on, Moon," Clint said, "don't turn on the old-man act. Use your memory."

"All right, all right," Moon said. He closed his eyes and then gave Clint an even more detailed description of Bonner than Clint had given him of the other three. Clint stared at the man, stunned.

"I ain't all gone in the head, ya know," Moon said with a wink. "Meet ya back here and we'll, ya know, compare notes."

Clint watched the old man cross the street and could have sworn there was a spring in his step.

Clint covered his side of the street quickly, stopping and looking in a saloon, a hardware store, a restaurant—he declined a table and said he'd return later—a gun shop, and a men's clothing store. He even stopped and looked in the window of a woman's clothing store. He doubled back then, passing the hotel and checking the other side of town with the same result.

When he returned to the hotel, prepared to wait for Moon, he found the older man sitting in a chair, waiting for him.

"How is it you can always find a chair?" Clint asked.

Moon grinned and said, "I had the young feller behind the desk carry it out for me so I could rest my frail bones."

"And what did your frail bones and you find?"

"Nothin'," Moon said. "You?"

"The same," Clint said, frowning.

"Don't mean nothin'," Moon said. "It's early, they could be indoors. Tonight we can check the saloons and the whorehouse."

Clint hadn't seen a whorehouse.

"You found the whorehouse?" he asked.

"First place I checked," Moon said. "There was three or four of them women wanted to get their hands on me, but I tole them I'd have to come back later and they'd all get a turn."

Clint decided that he'd *better* not take Moon up on his bet.

"Can we get a drink now?"

Clint looked at Moon and said, "You're not going to start anything, are you?"

Moon looked annoyed and said, "How many times I gotta say that waren't my fault?"

"Until I believe it," Clint said, "which is never. Come on, we'll go find a saloon, but if you open your mouth to do anything but put beer in it, I'm going to put my foot in it. You got that?"

"Yer threatenin' an old man," Moon said accusingly.

"That's right," Clint said, "I am."

TWENTY-FIVE

They went to the nearest saloon, ordered a couple of beers, and sat at a back table. The saloon was not filled even though it was early evening, and the men who were there were involved in their own drinks, or their own conversations.

"This may be the way we're going to have to play it," Clint said.

"How?"

Clint shrugged and said, "Just by sitting here and waiting for one of the four men to walk in."

"We better check and see how many other saloons are in town," Moon said. "If there are more than two, then how can we cover them all?"

"We can't," Clint said, "but I doubt that this town has more than two saloons."

"Well, there's always the whorehouse."

"Moon," Clint said, "somehow I think I'm going to have to keep you away from the whorehouse, just for your own good."

"You'll be protecting those gals more'n you'll be protecting me."

"I'm not going to argue this with you, Moon," Clint said.

"That's a switch."

Clint decided to remain silent on the subject.

"If we even had a name," Clint said instead, "we could go around and ask about him."

"That might not be so smart, either."

"Why not?" Clint thought he *knew* why not, but he liked the infrequent times when Moon decided to stop playing senile and make some sense.

"If they head right back here from that bank robbery—or any bank robbery—then this must be their home base. More than that, Testimony might even be their home. They're probably known here. I don't think we're gonna get much help here, Clint."

"You have a good point."

"Thanks."

Clint played with the beer mug on the table, making wet circles or just turning it around and around.

"You any good at waitin'?" Moon asked.

"Ordinarily," Clint said, "yes."

"What's that mean?"

"I'm anxious about this, Cole," Clint said, "real anxious . . . *too* anxious."

"There ain't nothin' wrong with that," Moon said. "I can unnerstand it."

"Thanks."

"What you gotta do is take it and put it away somewhere," Moon said. "Put it somewhere you can't find it, and it won't get in the way."

Clint stared across at Cole Moon and said, "You're pretty smart for a senile old man."

Moon grinned and gulped his beer down.

"Finish yours and I'll get two more."

Moon got up and walked to the bar. Clint lifted his beer mug to finish it, and then noticed the girl approaching him.

THE ROAD TO TESTIMONY

She and two other girls had apparently just come to work. This one wasn't young, probably in her late twenties, but she had the skin of a young girl, white and smooth, and plenty of it was showing at the neck of her red dress. She had long brown hair and a willowy figure, except for an excellent set of breasts. They were almost pear-shaped, which gave her a deep, shadowy cleavage.

"Can I get you something, mister?" she asked.

"Thanks," Clint said, "my friend is getting us a couple of beers."

"I wasn't talking about beer," she said, pressing her hip against his left shoulder.

"Uh, not right now," he said, "but maybe later."

"Well," she said, removing the pressure of her warm hip, "my name's Nellie. You want anything—even if it's another drink—just give me a call."

"I will, Nellie."

She walked away and he watched her admiringly. She knew how to walk to attract attention. Along the way she passed Moon, who almost walked into a chair because he was trying to look down her dress. Luckily he didn't spill a drop of beer.

"Did you see that gal?" he asked, sitting down and pushing a beer across to Clint.

"Yes," Clint said, "she was over here hawking her wares."

"Her wares?"

"Her charms."

"You mean she was tryin' to sell herself to you?" Moon said.

"That's right."

"Well, why didn't you say so?" Moon asked. "And why'd you let her get away?"

"I never pay for it, Moon."

"Pay for what?"

"Women."

"Why the hell not?" Moon asked. "What else is money for?"

"It's not for buying women," Clint said. "Not for me, anyway. Well, most always anyway."

"Why not?" Moon asked, frowning. "A woman is a woman, whether you paid for her or not."

"Moon," Clint said, very sure that he'd never be able to explain his feelings to the older man, "it's just not for me."

"Well, it is for me," Moon said. "Call her back over here."

"We've got other things to do," Clint said.

"Like what?"

"Like finishing these beers and doing what you suggested."

"What did I suggest?" Moon asked, as if he honestly couldn't remember.

"That we check the town for other saloons."

"Oh, that," Moon said, making a face.

Moon turned to see where Nellie was, and instead one of the other girls moved past, smiling at him. She was older than Nellie, about thirty-five, plump, and blond.

"Whoo-ee," Moon said, shaking his head. "Now, there's a lady with experience."

He turned and said to Clint, "Guess there'd be no harm in comin' back here later, would there?"

"Knowing you," Clint said, "probably."

As they left the saloon Moon said, "You ain't never gonna let me forget what happened in Palmeiro, are ya?"

"I just don't want it to happen again, Moon . . ."

TWENTY-SIX

Doing a survey of the town, Clint and Moon discovered that there was only one other saloon there. It was called the Lucky Lady. The saloon they had been in was called the Broken Branch. The Lady was a larger saloon, with more girls, more tables, and more house games.

"If we're gonna find them anywhere," Clint said, "this would be my guess. Those fellers are going to be guys who like the action."

"Well," Moon said, "then you wait here for them, and I'll wait at the other saloon."

Moon had already said that he preferred the girls at the other saloon to the girls at this one.

When they walked in he had looked at them and said, "These gals are bored with their work. Look at their faces. They don't even smile. Gimme the girls at the other saloon. At least they smile."

"All right, Moon," Clint said. "You can cover the other saloon, but don't get so interested in the girls that you forget why you're there."

"I know why I'm here, Clint," Moon assured him, turning serious.

"Well . . . don't get into any fights."

"I'll be careful, Papa."

"Yeah," Clint said, "that, too."

"I'll see you back at the hotel," Moon said.

"Make it about eleven—if you can stay up that long, old-timer."

Moon glared at Clint and said, "I'll be up long after you go to bed and long before you get up."

As Moon left, Clint was sure that the man was right. Clint's back was aching, and he looked around for a place to sit. He groaned to himself when he saw that there were no empty chairs—and then he saw one, at a table where four men were playing poker. He hadn't played poker in a while, his back *was* hurting, and he wouldn't stand out so much as a stranger if he was in a poker game.

He walked to the table and watched the end of the hand that was in progress, but before he could request permission to sit in, one of the players looked up and asked, "Care to take a hand?"

"I wouldn't mind," Clint said. "I need something to pass the time."

"Sit in, then, stranger," another man said. "That's just what we're doing, playing small stakes to pass the time."

Clint sat and the first man, who was shuffling, asked, "What's your name?"

"Cullen."

The man waited, then while dealing a hand of five-card draw asked, "Just Cullen?"

"That's it."

The man shrugged and set the remainder of the cards down on the table. Clint picked up his hand and found himself looking at absolutely nothing. When the play came to him he said, "I fold."

"I thought you needed somethin' to pass the time," a third player said to him.

THE ROAD TO TESTIMONY 103

Clint gave the man a baleful stare and said, "That doesn't mean I'm going to throw my money away while I'm doing it."

Over the course of the first hour of play that he was in the game, Clint could see that the third player was the kind of man who *never* sat out a hand. That was why he couldn't understand Clint's folding without even drawing a card.

The first player, the one who had invited him, seemed to be the best player in the game. His name was McCarthy. The second player, on Clint's right, was called Rusty. He was prematurely bald, but his eyebrows were red, so it wasn't hard to figure out where the name came from.

The third player—just to Clint's left—who sat in every single hand was called Blinky, for some reason Clint couldn't fathom. It seemed to him that the man *never* blinked, because he was afraid he'd miss something.

The fourth and last player, who had a sleepy style that was probably designed to put other players at ease, was named— of all things—Darling, and he seemed to have a good sense of humor about the name. He allowed the others to throw jibes at him, because while they were doing it, he was taking their money.

Apparently, before Clint had sat down, McCarthy and Darling had been doing all the winning. Now Clint was doing his share, while Rusty and Blinky continued to lose.

Blinky lost because he didn't know when to quit. Rusty seemed to be losing because of a run of bad luck. He came in second in three successive hands to McCarthy, Darling, and Clint.

"Luck's got to change sometime," McCarthy said to Rusty.

"Maybe," Rusty said. "I could also leave and come back another day."

"Come on," Blinky said, "don't break up the game."

"Plenty of butts around for his chair," Darling said. "Sometimes it's best to sit out a bad run of luck."

"I'll give it another hour or so," Rusty said.

As it turned out, his luck changed during that hour, and at one stretch he took three hands out of four. Clint took the fourth one.

After three hours of playing, Clint was ahead about fifty dollars. Faces had drifted in and out of the saloon, but none was familiar to him.

At one point McCarthy, who seemed to notice everything, asked Clint, "Waitin' for someone?"

Clint looked at him and said, "I have a friend in town who might come looking for me."

McCarthy nodded, apparently satisfied with the reply.

Once or twice a girl came to the table to take drink orders. Clint ordered one beer the entire time he was there, and every so often the same girl would come and take the warm one away and replaced it with a cool one. She was in her midtwenties, with long black hair and a very slender body, with almost no breasts. When she walked away, though, you could see that she had a wonderful ass.

"Thanks, angel," he said each time, and she'd smile at him and touch his shoulder.

"Ever notice the way the Lord treated some women?" Rusty asked. He was more talkative now that he was winning.

"What do you mean?" McCarthy asked.

"Well, he gave some of them perfect bodies and plain faces. Others have pretty faces and terrible bodies. Take Lisa there. She's as flat-chested as a boy, but what a rear end the Lord gave her."

"You lookin' for the perfect woman," McCarthy said, "you're goin' to be lookin' for a long time."

"I got the perfect woman," Rusty said. "She's waiting for me at home."

"Your wife?" Darling asked, as if surprised.

"That's right," Rusty said, sticking out his chin. "What's wrong with my wife?"

"Nothing," Darling said. "That is, if you could get her to shut up for five minutes."

Rusty fell silent after that, fuming, and Darling looked at Clint and smiled.

"I can talk to him like that," he said, " 'cause his wife's my sister."

"I see."

"She don't talk *that* much," Rusty said.

"Jesus," Darling said, "the woman talks like you wouldn't believe."

"Let's play cards," Blinky said, annoyed at the chatter.

So they played cards for another two hours, and when the clock started creeping up on eleven Clint decided it was time to meet with Moon. He hoped the older man would have more news than he did.

He left the table with a promise to return the next night to give them a chance to get their money back.

When he left, he was a whole hundred dollars ahead.

TWENTY-SEVEN

When Clint reached the hotel, Moon wasn't in the lobby, so he assumed the old man was in his room. He went to the second floor and knocked on the door of Moon's room, which was right across the hall from his. He heard some movement inside and knocked again.

"Awright, awright," Moon's voice called from inside. "I'm comin'."

Clint waited, wondering if the old man could really have a girl in there.

When the door opened Moon was standing there, naked to the waist, his feet bare. His hair was flying around his head, and he glared at Clint.

"Weren't we supposed to meet here?" Clint asked, trying to see inside the room.

"I'm a little busy right now, lad," Moon said. "Could we talk in a little while?"

"Moon," Clint said, "you don't really have a girl in there, do you?"

Moon gave Clint a would-I-lie-to-you look, then opened the door wide enough for Clint to see the bed. On it was the chunky blonde from the Lucky Lady saloon. She was sitting on the bed, very patient and very naked. Her breasts were large and round, with hard pink nipples.

"Custer," she said, "I'm waiting."

Moon grinned at Clint, who said, "I guess if you had anything to tell me, you would have told me by now, right?"

"Right you are, lad."

"All right, then," Clint said. "We can talk in the morning."

"In the morning it is."

"Early," Clint added.

"Right," Moon said, "early."

Clint permitted himself to smile finally and said, "Have a good night, Moon."

"I intend to, lad, I intend to."

The door closed in Clint's face and he heard bedsprings creak from inside. The old man must have leaped from the door to the bed.

He went to his own room, hoping that the old geezer wouldn't have a heart attack.

"You know," the blonde said to Moon, "for an, uh, older man you sure do have a long dick."

"Just imagine how long it was when I was younger," Moon said.

The blonde, whose name was Kim, was on her knees in front of Moon, who was sitting on the edge of the bed. She had one hand around his dick, down at the base, and with the other she was fondling his balls. She leaned forward and ran her tongue along the underside of Moon's dick, which twitched appreciatively.

"Ah, girl, that's quite a tongue you've got there," he complimented her.

"If you think the tongue is good," she said, looking up at him mischievously, "wait until you get the whole mouth."

Without delay, she opened her mouth and descended on him,

taking as much of his dick into her mouth as she could. She then proceeded to suck him wetly, her head bobbing up and down while she continued to fondle his balls. Moon placed one hand on her head and one hand on the mattress behind him, leaned back, and closed his eyes, surrendering himself to her marvelous mouth.

Later, Moon was lying on his back with Kim astride him, his rigid cock stuffed up inside of her. She was riding him enthusiastically, marveling at how soon the old man had been able to get it up again.

Moon's hands were greedily squeezing her tits, pinching the nipples, and she had her hands braced on his skinny stomach, riding him up and down as hard as she could. When she came down on him she jarred the bed, and it felt to her like his dick went all the way up between her breasts.

"Oh, shit . . ." she said as she started to come. She had been with a dozen men this week, and none of them had made her come like this. "Oh, Christ, I'm coming, Custer, Jesus, ain't I coming!"

"Well, wait for me, girlie," Moon said with a gasp. "I'll come with you!"

Even across the hall, Clint heard the woman's yell and Moon's bull-like bellow, and shook his head. Cole Moon continued to amaze him more and more.

"Custer?"
"Yeah?"

They were lying together on the bed, and she had one hand lolling lazily in his crotch.

"What are you and your friend doin' in town, hmm?" she asked.

"Can't tell you that, love," Moon said, his eyes closed. Her hand on him was, even to his surprise, starting to make him stiffen again. "It's a secret."

"Come on," she said, kissing his chest, "you can tell Kimmie."

She kissed his chest again, then licked it, and before long her wet mouth and eager tongue were all over him. Moon was skinny, but for an old man he didn't have a bad body. She was down between his legs now, licking his thighs and flicking his penis teasingly.

"Custer?"

"Mmm?"

"Come on, Custer," she said, licking his shaft, "tell me. . . ."

"Kim . . . I can't . . ." he said, panting, but before he could go any further her mouth engulfed him. Her head was moving over him, her mouth sliding up and down slickly, and just when he was about to blow his stack she took her mouth off of him and closed her hand around the base of his cock.

"Jesus . . ." he said, lifting his ass off the bed, "you gotta let me . . ."

"I'll let you have your pleasure," she said, running a nail over his long dick, " . . . as soon as you satisfy my woman's curiosity."

"Jesus," he said, straining off the bed, "finish me off, woman, and I'll tell you anything!"

"Custer—"

"Yer gonna give me a heart attack like this!"

"Oh, all right," she said, "but do you promise?"

"Hell, yeah, I promise!"

"All right," she said. Her wet mouth came down on him, and in moments he was exploding into her talented mouth.

Clint stood by his window and stared out at the dark street below. His mind was a jumble of frustrating thoughts, and they all started with "What if . . . ?"

What if the men who backshot him weren't here in Testimony? What if they were never coming here? What if Polly Haskell had simply heard wrong? What if this was all just a waste of time, and the trail was totally and completely cold?

What if Moon got a heart attack while he was in his room with that whore? Would that be his fault?

If anything good had come out of this, Cole Moon seemed to have come alive anew, and that was fine for him, but what about Clint himself? Ever since Hickok had been shot in the back and killed, Clint Adams's private demon had been the same thing happening to him. Now it *had* happened to him, and he had survived it. Should that be enough? If the answer was yes, he couldn't accept it. It was *not* enough that he had survived it. The only thing that would satisfy him now was avenging it.

If he couldn't do that, he didn't know what good he would be to anyone, ever again.

TWENTY-EIGHT

In the morning there was a knock on Clint's door. He rolled out of bed, wincing at the ache in his back, and walked, stooped over, to the door. When he opened it Cole Moon was standing there with a big smile on his face.

"I feel good today, boy," he said. "You ready for breakfast?"

"Come on in," Clint said. "Just give me a minute to straighten up."

"Back's bad this morning, huh?" Moon asked.

"It'll be fine," Clint said, straightening slowly.

"You know what'd be good for that?" Moon said. "Some of what I had last night. Get yourself a woman, boy."

"I don't need advice from you about women, Moon," Clint said. "Look, why don't you go downstairs and start breakfast and I'll join you."

"All right," Moon said, opening the door again. "I can see you ain't in a very good mood this morning."

"We'll talk downstairs," Clint said.

Moon shrugged and left the room.

Clint straightened up the rest of the way, rubbing his back. He wasn't in a bad mood *this morning,* he was *still* in a bad mood from *last night*. He had thought that a night's sleep might make him look at things differently come morning, but that wasn't the case. He was still frustrated, and so he planned on giving Moon the chance to go his own way and no longer be involved in what was turning out to be something akin to a dog chasing his own tail.

Clint dressed and left the room, heading down to the dining room. Moon was right about one thing: If he'd had a woman during the night, he might be in a better frame of mind this morning.

"What are ya talkin' about?" Moon asked.

He was already into his breakfast when Clint arrived. Clint ordered eggs and ham, and told the waitress to bring a strong pot of coffee right away.

"There is a pot on the table, sir," she said. She was a gray-haired woman in her fifties who was already bored, and it was early in the morning.

"That's his pot of coffee," Clint said. "I want my own pot."

When she went off to get it, looking wounded, Clint told Moon that maybe they should go their separate ways. That was when Moon asked him what he was talking about.

"This thing might take forever, Moon," Clint said. "You might as well go and find yourself a job somewhere while you're still feeling feisty."

"You're damned right I'm feelin' feisty," Moon said. "You know, those last couple of months in Dogtown I didn't even *feel* like havin' a woman—and I don't know that I coulda done anything, anyway. The only reason I'm feelin' the way I'm feelin' is that you got me up off my duff and onto a horse again. So if you don't mind, I'll be in this thing for the long haul."

"Moon—"

"As long as yer lookin' for these jaspers," Moon said, "so am I. Am I bein' clear?"

"Yeah," Clint said, after a moment, "you're being clear. Thanks, Moon."

"I got somethin' to tell ya, anyway."

"You found something out last night?"

"Not what we was lookin' for," Moon said, "but maybe somethin'."

The waitress came with the coffee then, put it down heavily on the table, and stalked off.

"Biddy," Moon said.

"What'd you find out?"

"That gal I was with last night?"

"Yeah?"

"She was real interested in what we was doin' in town," Moon said.

"How interested?"

"*Real* interested," Moon said.

"What did you tell her?"

"I told her we were lookin' for work."

"Did she believe you?"

"I don't know," Moon said. "She put me in a position where she thought she had everythin' her own way. Maybe she believed me, but why was she so interested?"

"What's your guess?"

"Somebody's got her checkin' into strangers in town," Moon said.

"Why?" Clint asked. "They can't know that we're after them."

"Maybe we ain't the only ones after them," Moon said. "Maybe they been robbin' banks in other places, too, and they come back here after every job."

"And they make sure they pull their robberies far enough away from here."

"But they still got somebody—like whatshername, Kim—checkin' on strangers."

"I like it," Clint said after a moment. "That means that they might be away now, pulling a job somewhere."

"And all we got to do is wait on them," Moon said.

"As long as it takes."

"Here comes that old biddy with yer breakfast," Moon said. "You better eat it up. We likely got a long day and night ahead of us."

TWENTY-NINE

As it turned out, they had plenty of long days and nights ahead of them. They were in Testimony a full week and they still hadn't seen any of the four men they were looking for.

Moon continued to see Kim a few times a week. Clint kept playing cards at the Lucky Lady, but as far as female companionship was concerned, he ended up with the girl, Nellie, from the Broken Branch.

He spent the evenings at the Lucky Lady, but he started having an after-dinner beer at the Branch, sitting with Moon for a while, and Nellie usually came over and talked to him. At the end of the first week he took her back to his room with him after he left the Lucky Lady and she finished at the Broken Branch.

He was suspicious for a while, since she worked at the same place as Kim, but Nellie never did ask him why he and Moon were in town. That first night, though, she did ask him if Moon was his father.

"Hell, no," he said. "Why do you ask that?"

"It ain't often you see an older man and a young man as close as the two of you are, if they ain't related."

That took Clint back a bit. He hadn't particularly considered that he and Moon were close. Why did it look that way to her?

"We don't even know each other that long," he said, and then decided not to say much more. He was talking too easily to her, and maybe her style was different from Kim's. She might just be *letting* him talk . . . but after a while he disregarded that possibility as well.

Nellie was twenty-three, and she had been born in Testimony when it was still called Flatrock. Whether it was called Flatrock or Testimony, though, she was just like any other young woman—like Polly Haskell, from Dogtown—who had never been anywhere. She wanted to leave. Clint made sure that she understood that there was no chance he would take her with him when he left.

Right at the end of the first week Clint got a visit from the local law. His name was Sheriff Bill Reynolds. He was a typical small-town sheriff, in his thirties, maybe his second or third go-round as a lawman, first time out from behind a deputy's badge. He was a big man, over six-three, and had a big man's arrogance. Clint had known big men before, and a lot of them had confidence, but the ones with arrogance were the ones who were easy to dislike. They had a habit of thinking that their size and strength made them special. It was the same malady suffered by men with a lot of money.

He was waiting for Clint in the hotel lobby one afternoon, and stepped up to him as he entered.

"Mr. Cullen?"

"That's right."

"Mind if we have a little talk?"

"About what?"

Reynolds looked around and said, "Why don't we sit down?" In the hotel lobby there was a small sofa on which he had been sitting while waiting.

"I can talk standing up," Clint said.

"Okay," Reynolds said, "suit yourself. I generally leave strangers in town alone for a while, Mr. Cullen, but you and your friend—what's his name, Custer?—have been here a week, and all I see you doin' in sittin' in the bar or walkin' around town."

"Is any of that against the law, Sheriff?" Clint asked.

"Well, no, I can't say that it is. Just what is your business in town?"

"I don't have any."

"Well, then, what's your business?"

"Generally whatever I can scare up."

"Well," the sheriff said, "I don't really care what you do for a livin', Mr. Cullen, but there are a couple of things I don't like in my town."

"And what's that?"

"Troublemakers," Reynolds said, "and bounty hunters."

"Now, sheriff," Clint said, "what would a bounty hunter want in your town? You got anybody livin' here with a price on their head?"

"Even if I did," Reynolds said, "I wouldn't appreciate a bounty hunter comin' here gunnin' for them."

"You mean you protect criminals here?"

"I mean what I say, Cullen," Reynolds said. "I don't want no trouble out of you and the old man. I'll be watchin' you—and I'll be checkin' on you."

"Go ahead and check, Sheriff," Clint said, "and let me know if you find anything interesting."

"Oh, if I find out anything interesting, Cullen," Reynolds said, "you'll be the first to know about it. Count on that."

That night Clint warned Moon about the lawman.

"I seen him watchin' me once or twice," Moon said. "Figured he was watchin' you, too. I was waitin' for him to get to this. What's he like?"

"Big man, big talk," Clint said.

"I know the type."

Clint related the conversation word for word, and Moon raised his eyebrows when he came to the part about bounty hunters.

"You think he knows what those four do and protects them?" he asked.

"I don't know," Clint said. "Maybe they're paying him off, or maybe he really doesn't like bounty hunters."

"And troublemakers."

"Well," Clint said, giving Moon a hard look, "we're not going to make any trouble, are we?"

"Who, me?"

"At least," Clint said, "not until our friends get here."

"What do we do if the law sides with them?" Moon asked.

"As an old lawman you probably wouldn't want to go up against him, Moon."

"You wore a badge for a time, too, Clint," Moon reminded him.

"Not nearly as long as you have," Clint said, "and not for a lot of years. If push comes to shove with the sheriff, Moon, I'm not backing down. I want you to know that up front."

"Don't worry," Moon said, "I'll back you. If he's bought and paid for, he shouldn't be wearin' that badge, anyway."

"Agreed."

So now while watching for their quarry they had to suffer the scrutiny of the sheriff and, as it turned out, his deputy, a younger man cut from the same cloth.

That night Clint asked Nellie about the sheriff.

"Is he honest?"

"Well, I guess that depends on what you consider honest," she said.

"What's that mean?"

"He's not chargin' protection or anythin', if that's what you mean."

"But . . ."

"It ain't nothin' I can put my finger on," she said, "just a feelin' I got that he's out more for himself than he is for the town. I mean, once or twice I've seen men walk out of his jail when they should have been there longer, or maybe when they should have seen a judge first—but then I don't know that much about the law."

"What about the town fathers? The mayor? Are they satisfied with Reynolds?"

"Oh, yes, they're very happy with him."

"How long has he been sheriff?"

"About three years."

"Well, if you think there's something wrong with him, I'd be inclined to believe you, Nellie."

Clint liked Nellie. Although young, she had been working in the saloon for five years, and he thought she knew what was going on. He valued her opinion—or maybe it was just because she was supporting *his* feelings about the sheriff. Either way, he was bound and determined that the star on Reynolds' chest was not going to come between him and his backshooters.

THIRTY

Through two weeks Clint was several hundred dollars ahead in poker and had become accepted as a regular part of the game. Even the other players—McCarthy, Rusty, Blinky, and Darling—had stopped being curious about him.

Kim and Nellie generally waited for Moon and Clint to let them know that they wanted them to come back to their hotel with them at night. Clint was relieved to see that Moon either didn't want to or wasn't able to take Kim to his room every night. He didn't think he would have been able to take it if the old man was outperforming him sexually. Hell, he was outperforming him in every other way.

His back was still sore in the mornings when he woke up, and toward the nights after sitting in a hard chair at the poker table for long hours. He had become so resigned to the waiting, though, that he had done what Moon told him to do: He had taken his impatience and put it away somewhere. Having done that, he found it much easier to be patient—and this was obviously going to take a lot of patience.

He'd take root if he had to, but he wasn't leaving Testimony without his pound of flesh—and he refused to consider that they were in the wrong place.

It was the only lead they had, and it *had* to pan out.

THIRTY-ONE

"How long before we get back to Testimony?" Dick Wheeler asked.

Wheat gave Wheeler a sour look and said, "Four days, five at the outside."

"I don't know if Rich is gonna last that long."

Wheat looked over at where Rich House was lying, near the fire.

This job had gone bad, and while they were making their escape they had shot—maybe killed—two lawmen. In turn, Rich House had been gutshot, and Wheat didn't know how the little man had hung on this long.

"Nothin' we can do but keep movin'," Wheat said. Wheeler nodded and went back to his friend's side.

Del Beman came over and stood by Wheat.

"You still mad?"

"Damn it, Del," Wheat said, "you said this job would be easy."

"I didn't *know* they put on extra lawmen, Wheat," Beman said for the hundredth time. "If I had, I wouldn'ta let us ride in there like that."

"And we didn't even get anything out of it," Wheat said. That was his biggest complaint. House was gutshot, Wheat had been nicked on the left arm, the law had run them off, they had killed two lawmen—or had shot them, since they had no way of knowing whether the men were alive or dead—and they had ridden away empty-handed.

Plus there *had* to be a posse on their trail.

"Think they're still trailin' us?"

"They got to be," Wheat said. "We shot two lawmen, Del, maybe killed them. That kind of thing don't go down easy."

"Yeah, but we crossed two borders already. You think they followed us?"

"Probably," Wheat said, "and they're probably pickin' up more help—local law and all—along the way."

"We can't lead them back to Testimony, Wheat," Beman said. "Reynolds can't protect us from this."

"We ain't gonna lead them home, that's for damned sure," Wheat said, "even if we got to take longer gettin' there."

"Rich ain't gonna last—"

"Rich ain't gonna make it anyway," Wheat said harshly. "You seen gutshot men before, Del. How he's lasted this long I don't know."

"Just plain stubbornness, I guess."

"Stubbornness nothin'," Wheat said with distaste. "The little worm is too scared to die."

"Ain't we all, Wheat?" Beman asked.

Instead of answering, Wheat grabbed his rifle, said "I'll take the first watch," and walked away.

As Bill Wheaton walked away, Del Beman looked over to where Dick Wheeler was crouched over Rich House, trying to give his friend some comfort.

Beman had always considered that he and Wheat were friends, but if that was him lying over there, gutshot and dying, would Wheat be crouched over him, trying to give him some comfort? Or would he be doing it for Wheat? He didn't think so.

It came as a shock to Del Beman that he didn't *have* any friends, not even in Testimony. All he had there was his father, still running the general store even though he had been mayor for ten years. Being mayor meant more to his father than anything—including him!

Maybe, he thought, just maybe he had gotten all he could get out of his relationship with Bill Wheaton. Even though it had been Beman who had set this particular job up, Wheat was the one who was getting more wild, more out of control. They could have ridden out this time without killing anybody, but Wheat had started shooting, and then they had *all* started shooting, and most likely—when Rich House died— that would leave three men dead.

It was time to let Bill Wheaton go his own way, and maybe it was even time to leave Testimony behind as well.

Alone on watch, Wheat was thinking that maybe it was time for him to cut himself loose from House, Wheeler, Beman, and Testimony. Why he kept going back to Testimony he didn't know. It sure didn't have anything to do with his father and mother being buried near there. He hardly remembered his mother; she had died when he was very young. He always felt that his father blamed *him* for his mother's death, so the old man had never given him anything in the way of affection. He resented that for a long time, but then he realized that it had made him the man he was today, the man who took what he wanted. Maybe he owed his father for that, but not much *more* than that.

No, Testimony held nothing for him anymore. Even that whore Kim was getting fat, and he was ready to leave her behind with everybody else.

Time for Bill Wheaton to go his own way and make his own name, and the first thing he was going to do was tell the world that *he* killed the Gunsmith. True, it had been Del Beman who actually shot Adams, but it had been Wheaton who set it up, so it was he who should reap the glory from it.

There was no other way to look at it.

THIRTY-TWO

While Wheat and Beman were thinking of going their own ways, Clint was sitting in the Lucky Lady saloon with Jay McCarthy and Sam Darling. They were waiting for the other players to come in, Darling's brother-in-law Rusty, and the poorest player of the lot—and the sorest loser—Ed "Blinky" Gorman.

"Two weeks is a long time for somebody who just drifted in one day," McCarthy said to Clint.

"Your curiosity back, McCarthy?" Clint asked.

"Just makin' conversation, Cully," the man said.

"How about you?" Clint asked Darling. "You curious, too?"

"I stopped being curious about other people's business a long time ago, Cullen," Darling said.

"Sounds like a good practice," Clint said, looking at McCarthy. "You should try it sometime."

McCarthy spread his hands and said, "Okay, so I'll mind my own business."

At that point Rusty and Blinky walked in, and the game started up. Several times during the game, though, Clint caught McCarthy studying him. It occurred to Clint that although he had been playing poker with these gents for two weeks, he didn't know much about them. He didn't know what their relationships in town were, if any. He didn't even know what their jobs were. He hadn't asked, because he hadn't wanted *them* to ask him what he did.

From pieces of conversations, though, he had been able to piece together *some* things. It sounded to him like Jay McCarthy owned the town's newspaper. That might explain the man's curiosity.

Ed "Blinky" Gorman most likely owned the livery, although he didn't run it himself. He was never there when Clint or Moon went to pay for their horses' board.

Rusty sounded like he was either top hand or foreman on a nearby horse ranch.

The only one Clint hadn't been able to pick anything up on was Sam Darling. The man kept to himself, he was a good card player, and he was confident in himself in more ways than one—a man with his last name would *have* to be. Of the four, he was the one Clint found the most interesting and knew the least about.

But he wouldn't ask.

The next afternoon Clint took a walk around town, as he often did. Once during his walk he saw the sheriff's deputy watching him.

He was about to go to lunch at a small restaurant he had found to his liking when he saw Sheriff Bill Reynolds step out of a doorway. Reynolds looked both ways, but didn't see Clint as he stepped into the street and crossed over. Clint waited until the man had gone far enough away, then crossed over to see what storefront he had stepped from.

The sign on the window said THE TESTIMONY EAGLE. It was the newspaper office. Clint moved to the window to peer in, and he saw Jay McCarthy inside. There were three men there, and McCarthy was the only one who wasn't covered with ink. Clint was sure that McCarthy owned and ran the paper.

He hadn't really looked at the newspaper since his arrival in Testimony, but he bought a copy now and took it to lunch with him. Sure enough, the owner/editor's name was J. McCarthy. McCarthy also did an editor's column, as well as some of the other stories—the ones that hadn't been picked up from other papers.

The Eagle looked like a competently put together newspaper. Clint put it down and applied himself to his lunch. He wondered how well Sheriff Reynolds and Jay McCarthy knew each other. He also wondered at the coincidence—and he absolutely *hated* that word—that had him in a card game with a man who had to be the most curious man in town. If he wasn't curious, why would he own a newspaper?

Clint finished lunch, and when he left he deliberately left the newspaper behind.

Later in the day, sitting in front of the hotel, he told Moon about McCarthy. While they were talking, the deputy was across the street, watching them. Clint smothered the urge to wave at the man.

"Man like that can't hold his curiosity in check for very long," Moon commented.

"And the sheriff did say he was going to check us out," Clint said.

"You think he's having this feller McCarthy do the checking?"

"It could be."

"So what?" Moon said, rubbing his hand over his jaw. "He sure ain't gonna find out anythin' about two yahoos named Cullen and Custer."

"No," Clint said, "and when he *doesn't* find out anything, that's just going to make him *more* curious."

"I see what you mean."

"We don't need the extra attention," Clint said.

"What do you plan to do about it?"

"I don't know yet," Clint said. "Maybe talk to one, or both of them, and give them something that will satisfy their curiosity."

"Like what?"

"I don't know what," Clint said. "If you think of something, let me know, will you?"

"Sure."

"You bringing Kim back to your room tonight?"

"Don't know as I feel up to it," Moon said. "My old bones is startin' to act up."

"Old bones, my ass," Clint said. "Is she still asking questions?"

"Once in a while," Moon said. "Like what are we still doin' here?"

"What are you telling her?"

"I'm tellin' her I don't know why *you're* still here, but she's the reason *I'm* still here."

"Does she believe that?"

"Shit, I dunno," Moon said with a grin. "I don't know what the bitch believes. All I know is I'm havin' the time of my life tryin' to *make* her believe it."

"Don't have a heart attack, old-timer," Clint said.

"No fear of that," Moon said. "She'll probably snap my old spine long before that happens."

THIRTY-THREE

Of course, it would have helped Clint and Moon if they could have heard the conversation between Sheriff Bill Reynolds and Jay McCarthy that afternoon.

"What do you mean, you can't find anything?" Reynolds asked McCarthy. "This fella Cullen has got to have either a reputation or a record."

"If he does, Bill, I can't find it," McCarthy said helplessly.

"And he doesn't let anything slip during the poker game?"

"He plays cards and watches everyone who comes into the place."

"He's here lookin' for somebody," Reynolds said. "He's a bounty hunter. I can see it in his eyes."

"Then why haven't we ever heard of him? Why hasn't *anyone* heard of him?"

Reynolds thought that one over for a few moments and then said, "Because he ain't usin' his real name, that's why."

"Why would a bounty hunter come to town under an assumed name?" McCarthy asked. In the privacy of his office McCarthy dropped the folksy accent he used when he was outside.

129

"Because whoever he's lookin' for, he don't want them to know it."

"All right, Bill," McCarthy said, "who's he lookin' for?"

"Who else could he be lookin' for, Jay?" Reynolds asked.

"Wheat?"

"That fool—we both know what he and Beman and those other two do when they leave here."

"Wheat's no fool, Bill," McCarthy said. "Even if they are breaking the law when they leave here, he'd never lead anyone back here."

"Obviously he didn't *lead* Cullen here, but the man found his way here anyway."

"No," McCarthy said, shaking his head.

"Yes," Reynolds said. "You wait and see. He's here for Wheat, and Beman, and the others."

"And if he is? What are you going to do?"

"Well, I can't let him take them, that's for sure," Reynolds said. "The old man wouldn't stand for it."

"Don't sell the old man short," McCarthy said. "Beman knows what kind of son he's got."

"Maybe so," Reynolds said, "but it's still his son. I'll have to talk to him about this."

"Go ahead, then."

Reynolds looked out the window. From where he was he could see the window to Mayor Beman's office, overlooking the street.

"What about the old man?" McCarthy asked.

"What about him?"

"If Cullen—or whoever he is—is a bounty hunter, what's the old man? His partner? That just doesn't make sense."

"I don't know," Reynolds said. "I guess that's somethin' else we'll find out."

Reynolds turned away from the window and looked at McCarthy.

"You know, I could *swear* I've seen Cullen before."

"Where?"

"I don't know," Reynolds said, shaking his head. "If only he didn't have all that hair all over his face."

"Yeah," McCarthy said, "and maybe that's *why* he's got all that hair all over his face."

"Yeah," Reynolds said, making a face as if he had just tasted something bad, "yeah."

He looked up at his boss's window again and said, "I hate this shit."

THIRTY-FOUR

Reynolds stood in front of Mayor Beman's desk and waited for the mayor to speak to him.

Beman had hired Reynolds three years ago with these words:

"You're the sheriff of Testimony, but you work for me. Can you handle that?"

"Yes, sir."

"What I say, you do," Beman had said. "What I say comes first, and this"—and he had held up the sheriff's star—"comes second. If you're the kind of lawman who thinks this"—again, the star—"is sacred, then you're not the man to work for me. Is this understood?"

"Yes, sir."

With that, Beman had tossed Reynolds the star and said, "Go to work."

Part of Reynolds' job for Beman was making sure nothing happened to his son Del. That was the part of the job that was starting to wear thin on him. He had accepted the job, with all its conditions, because he was tired of always wearing the deputy's badge and never the sheriff's star. This was his chance to be a sheriff, which was something he had wanted since he was very young. Lately, however, he was starting to think that perhaps he had traded too much for the hunk of tin he pinned to his chest every morning.

"Reynolds," Mayor Ted Beman said.

"Mr. Mayor."

"What's the problem?"

"There may not be one, Mr. Mayor, but . . ."

He explained to the mayor about the two strangers who were in town, and what he thought they might be in Testimony for.

"Have you seen my son?"

"No, sir. He still hasn't come back from his last, uh, trip."

"And you still can't figure out where you think you've seen this man before?"

"No, sir, not yet."

"What's his name?"

"Cullen?"

Beman wrote the name of a piece of paper.

"First name?"

"Nobody knows."

Beman looked up and frowned.

"Well, how did he register at the hotel?"

"Just as Cullen," Reynolds said, "from Texas."

"Does he sound like a Texan to you?"

"No, sir."

"I'll do some checking myself. Keep me informed."

"Yes, sir."

"You're the sheriff, Reynolds," Beman said. "I don't want these men to be here when Del *does* get back this time. Understand?"

"I understand, sir." Reynolds wondered what Ted Beman would do if Del Beman ever *didn't* come back from one of his trips.

"If you need more men, I can get them for you."

"I won't need any more men."

"That's all, then," Beman said. "Keep me updated. I'll be at the store."

Reynolds wondered about the store. Mayor Beman had plenty to do. So why did he insist on not only keeping the store but also working in it every day?

Reynolds had never known Beman when he *wasn't* mayor, so the man just didn't strike him as a storeowner. Ted Beman was in his late fifties, a big, barrel-chested man with slate gray hair and a stern face that sometimes looked like it had been chiseled from stone. This was not the kind of man Reynolds expected to find with an apron on behind the counter of a general store.

Reynolds backed out of the room, closing the door behind him. Beman had simply told him that he didn't want Cullen and the old man in town when Del came back. He didn't tell him how to go about it.

After the sheriff left, Ted Beman dropped his pen on his desk and turned in his swivel chair to stare out his window at the sky. He marveled at how perfect his life would be if it weren't for his son Del. Oh, he loved the boy and would protect him to his last drop of blood, but if only the boy would stop his traipsing around the country with his ne'er-do-well friends ... It was all that Bill Wheaton's fault. If only young Wheat would have grown up to be like his father, a simple farmer who never looked for trouble, instead of the hellion he turned out to be.

Beman stood up so he could look down at Testimony. This town had been built up from its Flatrock days due to his perseverance. He had gotten Western Union to put in a telegraph office, he had pursuaded Jay McCarthy to come here and start the *Eagle,* he had convinced the horsemen in the county to use

Testimony as a base for their business practices, and he had personally written to two eastern attorneys who specialized in that sort of business to come here to set up their practices. With all of the growing that Testimony had done over the years, he still had to keep a tight rein on his son and his friends so they wouldn't bring the whole thing tumbling down around him.

Sometimes he wished he had hired a more experienced lawman than Bill Reynolds, but Reynolds had had a good reputation as a deputy and had made no secret of the fact that he wanted to wear the sheriff's star. That gave Beman a carrot to dangle in front of the man's face so he could keep control of him.

Beman hoped that Reynolds would be able to handle the situation with this Cullen. If he couldn't, he was going to have to bring in outside help.

THIRTY-FIVE

"We oughtta turn the tables on them," Cole Moon said.

"What do you mean?" Clint asked.

"The sheriff's watchin' us, maybe we should be watchin' him," Moon said. "If he's protectin' these robbers, maybe he'll see them before we do."

"You know," Clint said, "that's not such a crazy idea. We could take turns keeping an eye on him."

"I'll start," Moon said. "I want to see the look on his face when he sees me followin' him."

"Follow him," Clint said, "but don't start anything with him."

"Who, me?"

"Don't play around, Moon," Clint said. "This sheriff has got something to prove, to himself and to the people of this town. I can see it in him."

"Don't worry," Moon said, "I ain't lookin' to get into a fight with him. He's a big fella. I'll leave that stuff to you."

"I'm not going to tangle with him unless I have to," Clint said.

"But you ain't backin' away from it, right?"

"I can't, Moon."

"I understand, Clint," Moon said, "believe me, I do. Once or twice I went huntin' for somebody for reasons of pure revenge."

"I don't like the word 'revenge,' " Clint said.

"What do you want to call it?"

"Justice."

"Your own special brand of justice, you mean?"

"I guess so."

Moon nodded and said, "I been down that road, too, a time or two."

"And what happened at the end of the road?" Clint asked. "Were you satisfied?"

"I can't tell you that," Moon said. "You got to find that out for yourself."

"That's fair," Clint said.

They were sitting in the Broken Branch over a couple of afternoon beers, and now Moon picked up his mug, drained it, and stood up.

"I'm gonna get started," Moon said.

"If the sheriff should approach you," Clint said, "just tell him to come and see me."

"I'll do that."

Clint watched Moon walk out. When the old man wasn't *playing* an old man, he was a downright comfort to have around.

A day's ride out of town, Bill Wheaton, Del Beman, and Dick Wheeler stopped to rest their horses. Beman looked over at Wheeler. Rich House had died two days ago, and Wheeler hadn't spoken a word to either one of them since. Neither of them had ever seen Wheeler this way, but then neither one of them had ever lost a close friend. Hell, neither one of them even *had* a close friend.

"We'll be in Testimony by noon tomorrow, Del," Bill Wheaton said. "When we get there we got some serious talkin' to do."

"That's funny," Beman said, "that's what I was gonna say to you."

"I guess maybe we both got the same thing in mind, huh?" Wheat asked.

"Probably."

When they had fled Missouri they'd crossed into Kansas, and then changed direction and crossed into Oklahoma. It was in Oklahoma that they managed to lose the posse that was following them. That done, they had headed directly for Texas. Since Rich House had died—and they had buried him— they had managed to make a lot better time.

Wheeler was off to the side, away from them, so he couldn't hear them talking.

"What do you suppose is goin' on in his head?" Del Beman asked.

"I never thought *anything* was going on in either one of their heads," Wheat said, "so I ain't about to start now."

"He must be hurtin'," Beman said.

"Stop thinkin' about it," Wheat said. "Let's keep movin'."

Wheat kicked his horse into a gallop and started ahead of Beman and Wheeler. Beman watched Wheeler and waited for him to move, then fell in behind him.

For some reason, he didn't want the quiet man riding behind him.

THIRTY-SIX

The look on Sheriff Reynolds' face when he saw the old man following him was everything Cole Moon had hoped it would be. He had to keep himself from cackling out loud.

Reynolds stood the tail for about three hours, but when he finally realized that no matter where he went, Moon was going to be there, he decided to do something about it.

Moon was surprised when the sheriff didn't approach him. The man led him around town, and it soon became obvious what the lawman was doing. He was looking for the man he knew as "Cullen."

Clint was in the Lucky Lady when Sheriff Reynolds entered. Clint was sitting at the poker table alone, as none of the other players had arrived yet.

"I want to talk to you," Reynolds said, confronting Clint.

Clint remained seated and said, "Go ahead, talk."

"You've got your old man tailing me all over town, and I don't like it."

"First of all, he's not my old man," Clint said. "Second of all, you've had you deputy tailing *us* for days, and you yourself have been watching us."

"That's our job."

"That's fine," Clint said. "Then while my friend is following you, you'll be able to keep an eye on him. It all works out for the best."

Reynolds opened his mouth to speak, then looked around them, noticing that they were the center of attention. He sat down then and lowered his voice.

"What do you think you're tryin' to do?"

"Just making it easy for you to know what we're doing, Sheriff," Clint said, spreading his hands. Beyond the sheriff's left shoulder he saw Jay McCarthy enter the saloon. The newspaperman stopped short when he saw the sheriff sitting with Clint, then changed his direction and headed for the bar.

"I'll tell you what will make that even easier, Cullen," Reynolds said. "You and your . . . friend have until tomorrow morning to leave town."

"We haven't broken any laws," Clint said. "You can't run us out of town."

"Sure I can," Reynolds said. "You've broken one of *my* laws."

"Which law is that, Sheriff?"

Reynolds leaned forward and said, "You tried to make me look like a fool in my own town. I don't stand for that, Cullen—or whatever your name is."

"What's that supposed to mean?" Clint asked, because it was the logical next question.

"I think you know what it means, mister," Reynolds said. "I've checked you out, and there's no record of you anywhere—under that name, that is. It's my bet that your real name is *not* Cullen, and if I had the time I'd find out what your name really is."

"If you weren't running us out of town," Clint said, "you'd have the time."

"Believe me, I'm tempted to let you hang around until I

do," Reynolds said, "but it's in *your* best interest to leave by tomorrow morning."

"I'll consider it."

"Do more than that, mister," Reynolds said. "Do a helluva lot more than that."

As Reynolds left, the others in the bar watched him go and then turned their attention to Clint, who ignored them.

Jay McCarthy carried two beers over to the table, set one down in front of Clint, and sat across from him.

"What was that all about?"

Clint sipped the fresh beer and then said to the newspaperman, "Somehow, I think you already know."

"What's that supposed to mean?"

"You been pumping me for information since the day I first got here," Clint said. "Oh, nothing obvious, but there are always the little questions you ask in that folksy way you have." Clint sat forward and asked, "Has that been for your own curiosity, or did the sheriff put you up to it?"

"I'm a newspaperman, Cully," McCarthy said. "Newspapermen ask questions. It's how I make my living."

"Is that right? The sheriff says he did some checking on me. I suppose you did, too?"

"I asked around."

"And?"

"And I can't find out a bloody thing about you—as Cullen, that is. Maybe if you gave us a first name it would help?"

"It wouldn't."

McCarthy suddenly looked interested, as if Clint had finally let something slip.

"Does that mean that Cullen *isn't* your real name?"

"It just means that my first name wouldn't help you," Clint said, "nothing more."

McCarthy opened his mouth to say something else, but at that moment the other players walked in.

"Can we talk tomorrow?" he asked, quickly. "In my office?"

"Sure," Clint said. "Why not?" He didn't tell McCarthy that he and Moon had been ordered out of town.

After that the others sat down, and the game started up. During the game Moon came in and jerked his head Clint's way.

"Excuse me a second, gents," Clint said, and walked to the bar.

"The sheriff went straight from here back to his office and he ain't been out since," Moon said with glee. "We sure spooked him."

"Yeah," Clint said, "so much so that he's ordered us to leave town."

"When?"

"By tomorrow morning."

"And we ain't, right?"

"Right."

"So I guess we'll find out somethin' about this sheriff tomorrow, huh?"

"I guess we will."

"You still want me to watch him?"

Clint hesitated a moment, then said, "No, I don't think so. We'll know where he is soon enough when he comes looking for us in the morning. Besides, our friendly newspaperman wants to talk to me tomorrow. Let's see what he has to say about all of this."

"Then I'll be at the Broken Branch."

"Okay."

"And I'll probably be bringin' little Kimmie back to my room tonight, seein' as how this might be our last night in town."

"Fine," Clint said. "I'll have the smelling salts ready."

THIRTY-SEVEN

Clint wasn't concentrating on the game, so he left the Lucky Lady early. He stopped by the Broken Branch to see if Nellie could leave early, and she was able to. Moon and Kim were still there, but he knew it wouldn't be long before loud noises were coming from Moon's room.

Clint was rougher that night with Nellie than he had been in the past, something he realized only after they'd had sex together. She was gasping for air when they were done, and he realized that even during sex he had virtually forgotten that she was there.

"I'm sorry," he said afterward.

"Don't apologize," she said, breathing hard. "It was . . . different, but it was still wonderful."

"No," Clint said, "I was . . . sort of lost there for a while."

"I guessed," she said. "I guess I could have been anybody tonight, huh?"

"Don't be insulted, Nellie—"

"I'm not insulted, Cullen," she said quickly, and he believed her. "I understand that men sometimes get frustrated and need to . . . to release the frustration. That's all right with me. I like you, and I want to help you."

"I just feel badly for . . . using you."

She kissed him and said, "You're a nice man, Cullen. Not many men would even worry about it."

"Well, I do."

"Maybe if you told me why you're frustrated," she said. When he didn't reply right away she asked, "Does it have something to do with this nasty wound on your back?"

Clint hesitated a moment and then said, "Yes, it does."

"Are you here lookin' for the man who did it to you?" she asked.

Clint looked at Nellie and wondered if she was now pumping him the way McCarthy had been doing, or the way Kim had done to Moon.

"What's wrong?"

"I'm just wondering if I can trust you."

She didn't become insulted.

"I can't tell you that, Cullen," she said. "That's up to you. I can tell you one thing, though."

"What?"

"Kim has a boyfriend that she worries about, and when strangers come to town she tries to find out what they're doin' here. That's why she's been spendin' so much time with your friend."

"I see."

"She wanted me to question you for her, but I wouldn't do it."

"Why is she so worried about her boyfriend?"

"Because he . . . he lives here, but he goes away for long periods of time, and then when he comes back he has . . . has lots of money to spend."

"And what do you think he's doing when he's away?"

"I think he's breakin' the law," she said. "You know, robbin' people, or even robbin' banks—"

Clint didn't know if he was going to be able to keep his

anxiety in check. He didn't want to scare her by showing her how important the things she was saying were.

"Who is her boyfriend, Nellie?"

"His name is Wheat," she said. "Well, they call him Wheat, but his name's Bill Wheaton." She sat up in bed and looked at him. "Is that who you're lookin' for?"

"I don't know who I'm looking for, honey," he said. "I don't have any names. Does Wheat have friends that he travels with?"

"Yes," she said, "three of them."

Now his heart was pounding.

"I'm looking for four men."

"My God," she said, "it was them that done this to you? They shot you in the back?"

"Who are they, Nellie? What are their names?"

"There's Wheat, Dick Wheeler, Rich House, and then there's Del Beman. He's Mayor Beman's son."

The mayor's son! That was it.

"That's why Reynolds wants to protect them," he said aloud.

"The sheriff will do anything the mayor tells him to do," Nellie said.

Clint's first inclination was to rush from the bed across the hall to tell Moon what he had found out, but he quickly realized that there was nothing they could do until morning. Also, why ruin Moon's enjoyment of Kim right now by telling him that she was this Bill Wheaton's girlfriend?

"Nellie," he said, "describe all four of these men to me."

From the descriptions she gave him he was certain that they were the men he was looking for. Also, he could tell that the only man he hadn't seen was Del Beman—because he had been *behind* Clint. It was Beman—the mayor's son—who had shot him in the back!

That was going to make taking them down a very interesting proposition.

"Nellie," Clint said, "will you tell me everything you know about these four men?"

"Is that what you want me to do?"

"That's what I want you to do . . . right now!" he said. "Later we'll do something else a lot nicer."

She smiled at him and said, "All right. Where shall I start?"

"Start with the mayor's son and work your way up," he said, then added to himself, or down.

THIRTY-EIGHT

Early the next morning Clint knocked on Moon's door, quietly but insistently. When Moon answered, Clint asked, "Is she still in there?"

"Yeah, wha——"

"We have to talk," Clint said, beckoning Moon out into the hall.

"I can't come out in the hall!" Moon said. "I'm nekkid!"

"Well, put something on and come to my room."

"What about Nellie?"

"She's gone." Nellie had left half an hour earlier, after they'd spent a good part of the night doing the "nice" thing.

"All right," Moon said. "I'll be there in a second."

Clint went back into his room and left his door ajar. True to his word, Moon entered seconds later.

Clint told Moon what he had learned from Nellie. When he was done, Moon said, "That blond bitch!"

"She was only trying to protect her man," Clint said. "Besides, you enjoyed her, didn't you?"

Moon stared at him for a moment, then chuckled and said, "I sure did."

"So, no harm done," Clint said. "At least now we know who we're dealing with."

"Yeah," Moon said, "the goddamn mayor of the town. How many deputies has that sheriff got?"

"One that I know of," Clint said, "and they're likely to be in the lobby when we go down this morning."

"We better come up with a plan."

"Well," Clint said, "here's what I had in mind, and it's fairly simple . . ."

When Clint went down to the hotel lobby it was no surprise to find the sheriff waiting there for him.

"Checking out, Cullen?"

"No, Sheriff," Clint said, "I was going to have breakfast. Care to join me?"

"Have breakfast on the trail," Reynolds said. "You're leavin'. Where's your friend?"

"I guess he must still be in bed," Clint said. "He brought a lady back with him last night."

"Get him down here."

"I wouldn't interrupt him, Sheriff," Clint said. "He gets real riled when he's with a lady and he's interrupted. Why, once he—"

"Never mind that," Reynolds said. "Get him down here."

"I'm already down here, Sheriff," Moon said from behind the lawman.

Reynolds moved for his gun, but Clint froze him by yelling, "Don't do it!"

Moon came into the hotel lobby, pushing the disarmed deputy ahead of him through the front doorway. Clint similarly disarmed the sheriff.

"You can't get away with this," Reynolds said. "I'm the law."

"We'll see how long that lasts when we get some federal help in here."

"Federal law?" Reynolds said. "For what?"

"I think they'd like to know that you use your badge for the benefit of Mayor Beman and his crooked son."

"Wha——"

"Oh, yeah," Clint said, "I know all about young Beman and his friends. You see, I had an experience with them firsthand."

"What are you talking about?"

"They shot me in the back and left me to die, and that was after they robbed a bank in Wyoming. I guess they figured to make a name for themselves by killing me, only it didn't quite work. It seems they decided to keep quiet about it."

Reynolds frowned and asked, "Why would killing you make a name for them? Who are you?"

"My name's Clint Adams, Sheriff."

Reynolds' reaction was immediate.

"The Gunsmith?"

"That's right," Moon said, "the Gunsmith."

"And they shot you in the back?"

"You know any other way they coulda taken him?" Moon asked.

"Actually," Clint said, "Wheaton, Wheeler, and House fronted me. It was your mayor's son, Del Beman, who pulled the trigger."

Clint was naming all the names so Reynolds would know that it was futile to lie.

"You'll never get out of this town alive, Cullen—I mean, Adams."

"You got that wrong, Reynolds," Clint said. "It's Del Beman, Bill Wheaton, and the others who'll never get out alive."

He gave the sheriff's gun to Moon and said, "Keep them here."

"Where are you goin'?"

"First I'm going to talk to the newspaperman, McCarthy. Then I'll go and talk to the sheriff's boss, the mayor himself."

"Be careful."

"Don't worry," Clint said. "Just keep these two here."

"How long do you think you can hold us?" Reynolds shouted.

Clint stopped at the door and said, "Just until the four men I want come back to town."

As Clint left he heard Reynolds shout, "What if they never come back?"

Outside, where only he could hear himself, Clint said, "Don't worry, they will."

THIRTY-NINE

Clint had to bang on the front door of the newspaper office to rouse McCarthy from his back room. The newspaperman came to the door belting his bathrobe and squinting at the door to see who it was.

When he opened the door McCarthy said, "What the hell—"

"You said you wanted to talk to me."

"Yeah, but I meant at a decent time—"

"Now's the time, McCarthy," Clint said, "unless you don't want to talk to me."

"All right, all right," McCarthy said, backing away from the door. "Tell me what's so urgent that we have to talk now."

Clint closed the door behind him and said, "My real name is Clint Adams."

"Clint . . . Adams?" McCarthy said. "You mean—"

"Yes, that's what I mean," Clint said.

"I heard you were dead."

"Right now my partner is holding the sheriff and his deputy at the hotel."

"At gunpoint?" McCarthy said.

"That's right," Clint said. "Do you want to write any of this down?"

"This is all for publication?" McCarthy asked, surprised.

"Every word," Clint said. "Consider this an interview."

McCarthy rooted around until he found a pad of paper and a pencil.

"Why are you holding the sheriff and his deputy?" McCarthy asked anxiously.

"Let me tell it my way," Clint said. He told McCarthy what had happened in Wyoming, and how he had tracked the men who shot him here. He now knew the names of the four men, and he was convinced that they were on the way here.

He told McCarthy that the mayor and the sheriff have been protecting men who were most likely wanted in any number of other states.

"And you're going to take them in?" McCarthy asked.

"I'm going to make sure they never shoot another man in the back again," Clint said. "That's the end of the interview."

"Wait," McCarthy said. "What are you going to do to them?"

"I have to go."

"Where?"

"To talk to the mayor."

"Do you know where he lives?" McCarthy asked.

Clint stopped at the door and turned to face McCarthy.

"No."

"Let me get on a pair of pants and I'll take you to his house."

McCarthy ran into his back room without waiting for Clint to comment.

"There's the house," McCarthy said.

It was the biggest house Clint had seen since his arrival in town, and it was obviously a fairly new structure.

Clint mounted the porch and began pounding on the mayor's

THE ROAD TO TESTIMONY   153

door. McCarthy stood off to the side, prepared to watch and listen.

When the door was finally opened the man standing in the doorway was livid.

"What the hell—McCarthy, is that you?"

"Mayor Beman?" Clint said.

"What? Who are you? McCarthy?"

"McCarthy is just here to listen and watch, Mayor," Clint said. "You'll direct your comments to me."

"What?"

"My name is Clint Adams," Clint said, "although you might know me better as Cullen."

"Cullen!" the mayor said, taking a step back. "Wait a minute. Did you say . . . Clint Adams?"

"That's right."

"Where—where is the sheriff?"

"He's busy," Clint said. He entered the house, and the mayor took as many steps back as he had to to avoid contact. McCarthy came in behind them.

"What's going on?"

"Dear?" a woman's voice called from upstairs. "Who is it?"

"Don't let her come down here," Clint said.

"Stay upstairs, Emma," Mayor Beman said. "I'll be up soon."

Clint waited to see if the woman would come down anyway, and was satisfied when she didn't.

"What's going on?" Beman demanded. "What do you want here?"

"I came to deliver a message," Clint said. "Your days of covering for your son and his friends are over."

"Covering—"

"Let's not play games, Mayor," Clint said. "Your son and

his friends shot the wrong man in the back."

"What?"

"That's right," Clint said. "They shot me in the back and left me for dead, and guess what? I didn't die. Now I'm back, and it's time for justice to rear its lovely head."

"Justice? What are you—where's the sheriff?"

"The sheriff and his deputy are busy at the moment. They won't be able to help your son and his friends, and neither will you."

"I won't let anything happen to my son, Adams," Beman said. "I can promise you that."

"I sympathize with your plight as a father, Mayor," Clint said, "but unless you're as crooked as your son is—"

"I am an honest man, sir!"

"Please, Mayor," Clint said, "you're a politician."

"I don't think—"

"That's enough," Clint said. He turned to look at McCarthy and said, "You got enough for a story?"

"I've got plenty."

"McCarthy, you can't write this up."

"Mr. Mayor, you asked me to come to this town and edit a newspaper," McCarthy said, "and that's what I'm going to do."

"You'll never edit another newspaper, McCarthy!" Beman shouted.

"I'll take that chance, Mayor," McCarthy said. "How many opportunities will I have to print a headline like '*MAYOR COVERS FOR KILLER SON*'?"

"What? Killer—you can't!"

"Let's go, McCarthy," Clint said. "I'll be standing by Mr. McCarthy while he typesets this story, Mayor. You send any guns against him, they're going to have to deal with me."

Clint turned and left the mayor's house, with McCarthy close behind him.

Clint stopped short, so short that McCarthy almost walked into him.

"Why do I have the feeling this is all going to come to an end today?" Clint asked.

FORTY

True to his word, Clint stood by McCarthy while he set the type for the story that would appear in that day's newspaper.

"You know, this is going to make it more difficult for you to stay here and wait for Beman, Wheat, and the others to come back."

"I don't think so," Clint said.

"Why not? You can't hold the sheriff forever. The mayor is bound to send someone after you. What if it takes another couple of weeks—"

"I told you outside the mayor's house," Clint said. "Everything is coming to a head today."

"What makes you say that?"

"I can feel it," Clint said, and he could. Ever since last night, when Nellie had told him about Kim's boyfriend, he had felt this whole thing snowballing.

"You don't have to stay here, you know," McCarthy said. "I'll be fine. You better check on the sheriff and his deputy."

"If I know Moon, he's got them in their own jail by now," Clint said.

McCarthy stopped short and said, "Moon?"

"That's his real name."

"Not . . . *Cole* Moon?"

"That's right," Clint said, "Cole Moon."

"Jesus," McCarthy said, "Cole Moon *and* the Gunsmith. What a story!"

"You'll have to talk to Moon to see if he wants to be in your paper," Clint said.

"Well, let's go and talk to him!"

They checked the hotel first, but as Clint had suspected, Moon had taken the sheriff and the deputy and put them in their own jail. When Clint and McCarthy entered the sheriff's office they could hear Reynolds shouting from a jail cell.

"What's going on?" Moon asked.

"I've told Mr. McCarthy the whole story, Moon, and he wants to write it up in his newspaper. He wants to know if he can use your name in the story."

"I'd like to do a sidebar story on you, Clint, and one on you, Mr. Moon."

"Just Moon, sonny."

"I feel like I should call you Marshal Moon."

"Those days are long gone," Moon said, "but sure, use my name in your story."

"It's getting late," Clint said, "almost eleven. When can you have this newspaper out by?"

"It'll be on the street by two."

"That'll have to do."

"Can Marshal Moon come back to the office with me?"

Clint looked at Moon, who said, "Sure, if Clint stays here."

"Great!"

"The man's gonna make stars out of us, Clint," Moon said.

"Not in *The Testimony Eagle,* Moon," Clint said.

If McCarthy heard the comment, he didn't react, and he and Moon went out the doorway.

"Adams!" Reynolds shouted. "You won't get away with this!"

"Shut up!"

"We're home," Wheat said.

"For as long as it will still be home," Beman said.

They both sat and stared at the town of Testimony, while Dick Wheeler stayed off on his own.

"We really are thinkin' the same thing, ain't we?" Wheat said. "We've both had enough of Testimony."

"And each other," Beman said.

"Yeah," Wheat said, "yeah, I guess . . ."

"Come on," Beman said, "let's get this over with."

"Gonna tell Daddy right away?" Wheat asked as they started riding.

McCarthy and Moon were crossing the street back to the sheriff's office when the three riders appeared on the street. Somehow, word had gotten out that something was going to happen today, because the street was pretty empty.

"Jesus," McCarthy said.

Moon, looking off down the street, said, "Is that them?"

"Yep," McCarthy said, "that's them. Sonofagun, Adams was right. This is gonna end today."

"I hope," Moon said.

"Why is the street so empty?" Wheat wondered out loud.

"Somethin's wrong here," Beman said.

Dick Wheeler also wondered what was happening, but he kept his mouth shut.

Mayor Beman had left his house and gone to his office, because he didn't know what else to do. He hadn't even explained to his wife what was happening. He felt safe in his

THE ROAD TO TESTIMONY

office, and now from the window he saw his son Del riding in with Wheaton and Wheeler. He was so worried about what was going to happen that he didn't even notice that Rich House wasn't there.

He put his hand on the window and opened his mouth, as if to shout to his son, but then he realized that no one would be able to hear him.

He turned to leave his office, but stopped even before he could come out from behind his desk. He had been protecting his son for years, many years now, and now maybe it was time for him to stand up for himself.

He turned and looked out the window again and held his breath.

Moon walked to the sheriff's office, opened the door, and said to Clint, "They're here."

FORTY-ONE

Clint came out onto the street and saw the three riders, who had stopped farther down the street.

Jay McCarthy crossed back to his office and stood on the boardwalk in front of his window to watch. This was why he had become a newspaperman.

"I don't know what's goin' on," Wheat said, "but I don't like it."

From his horse, Beman could see the window of his father's office, and he saw his father standing there, watching.

"Where is everybody?" Wheat asked.

"And who's this?" Beman asked.

Ahead of them a man had walked to the center of the street and was now walking toward them. He had long hair and a shaggy beard, but there was something familiar about him.

"He don't look like a lawman," Wheat said.

"Let's find out just who he *is*," Beman said.

None of the three saw Moon, who was walking just behind Clint, on the side of the street to their right.

THE ROAD TO TESTIMONY

• • •

Clint stopped about twenty feet away from the three men.

"Where's the fourth man?" he asked. "House, was it?"

"Who the hell are you?" Wheat asked.

"My name is Clint Adams," Clint said.

"What?" Beman said.

"You can't be," Wheat said.

"Why?" Clint asked. "Because you killed me?" He looked at Beman and said, "You're the one I didn't see. You put the bullet in my back, didn't you?"

"Jesus," Beman said.

"You're dead," Wheat said.

Clint looked at Wheeler and said, "What's your say in this?"

Wheeler spoke for the first time since Rich House died.

"My friend is dead," Wheeler said. He used his left hand to remove his gun from his holster and dropped it to the ground. "I'm ready to turn myself in."

"Get off your horse and get off the street," Clint said.

Wheeler obeyed, dismounting and moving off the street.

Clint looked at Beman and Wheat and spoke to them in turn.

"You put the bullet in my back," he said, "but I'd bet it was your idea, wasn't it?"

"It *was* my idea," Wheat said, "and I should have gotten credit for it."

Clint looked at Beman and said, "It was your idea not to brag about it."

"It was a stupid thing to do," Beman said, "and it would have been even more stupid to brag about it."

"You *know* it was stupid, and yet you pulled the trigger?"

Beman opened his mouth, and then shook his head helplessly. He couldn't think of anything to say to the man he had shot in the back and left for dead.

"Shit," Wheat said, "this is bull. You ain't the Gunsmith, and I'm gonna prove it."

"How are you going to do that, Wheat?"

"By killin' you!"

Wheat grabbed for his gun, absolutely sure that he could outdraw this pretender. He was still sure of it when Clint's bullet struck him in the chest and knocked him from his horse.

Del Beman immediately thrust his hands into the air and said, "Don't shoot."

Clint walked right up to Beman's horse, so close to the man that he could see him sweating. He extended his gun, pointing it right at Beman's face.

"Don't," Beman said, "don't . . ."

"Maybe I should make you turn around," Clint said. "What do you think, Del?"

"Adams," Beman said, "don't . . . I'm sorry, I'm sorry . . ."

"How many men have you and your friends killed on these . . . these trips of yours, Del? Are you sorry for all of them?"

"Adams," Beman said, "my father's the mayor. He'll give you anything."

"Really?"

Clint turned his head just a bit, so he could look up at the mayor's window. Mayor Beman was still standing there, watching.

"I don't see your old man running down here to help you, Del," Clint said. "I think you're on your own now."

"God . . ." Beman said.

From behind Clint both Moon and McCarthy approached.

"Don't do it, Clint," Moon said.

"When my paper comes out, Adams, they're finished," McCarthy said. "Him *and* his father."

Clint cocked the hammer on his double-action Colt unnecessarily, and Beman flinched.

"Clint," Moon said, "people are startin' to come out. There's too many witnesses. If you kill him it'll be *murder*."

"This is the end of the trail I was asking you about, Moon," Clint said. "How do I satisfy myself? How do I come out of this happy?"

"You don't do it by doin' what he did," Moon said. "You don't do it by becomin' a killer."

"That's already my rep, isn't it, Moon? A killer? The Gunsmith?"

"Maybe, son," Moon said. He was so close to Clint now that his mouth was right in Clint's ear. "But you ain't never been accused of killin' anybody in cold blood."

Clint stared up at Beman, whose eyes were closed. Sweat was dripping off his chin. Suddenly Clint reached up, grabbed the front of the man's shirt, and pulled the man from the saddle. Beman fell to the ground hard, and Clint pointed his gun at him, *wanting* to pull the trigger.

"Make a grab for your gun, Del," he said, "please."

"I—I ain't," Beman said, pushing his hands straight out ahead of him as he sat in the dirt, "I ain't . . ."

Clint put the barrel of his gun right against the man's forehead, counted to ten, and then moved the gun away. He pushed the hammer off cock and holstered the gun.

"Put him in a cell, Moon," he said. "I'll go to the telegraph office and send for some federal law to clean up Testimony."

"You've already done that, Clint," Jay McCarthy said. "They'll just be picking up the pieces."

Clint walked away from Del Beman, the man he badly wanted to kill, and the farther he got from the man, the better he felt about *not* having done so.

And for the first time in over three months, he felt *better*.

Watch for

THE WITNESS

131st novel in the exciting GUNSMITH series
from Jove

Coming in November!

SPECIAL PREVIEW!

Giles Tippette, America's new star of the classic western, tells the epic story of Justa Williams and his family's struggle for survival . . .

Gunpoint

By the acclaimed author of *Sixkiller, Hard Rock* and *Jailbreak*.

Here is a special excerpt from this riveting new novel—available from Jove Books . . .

I was standing in front of my house, yawning, when the messenger from the telegraph office rode up. It was a fine, early summer day and I knew the boy, Joshua, from a thousand other telegrams he'd delivered from Blessing, the nearest town to our ranch some seven miles away.

Only this time he didn't hand me a telegram but a handwritten note on cheap foolscap paper. I opened it. It said, in block letters:

I WILL KILL YOU ON SIGHT JUSTA WILLIAMS

Joshua was about to ride away on his mule. I stopped him. I said, "Who gave you this?" gesturing with the note.

He said, "Jus' a white gennelman's thar in town. Give me a dollar to brang it out to you."

"What did he look like?"

He kind of rolled his eyes. "I never taken no notice, Mistuh Justa. I jest done what the dollar tol' me to do."

"Was he old, was he young? Was he tall? Fat?"

"Suh, I never taken no notice. I's down at the train depot

an' he came up an ast me could I git a message to you. I said, 'Shorely.' An' then he give me the dollar 'n I got on my mule an' lit out. Did I do wrong?"

"No," I said slowly. I gave his mule a slap on the rump. "You get on back to town and don't say nothing about this. You understand? Not to anybody."

"Yes, suh," he said. And then he was gone, loping away on the good saddle mule he had.

I walked slowly back into my house, looking at the message and thinking. The house was empty. My bride, Nora, and our eight-month-old son had gone to Houston with the balance of her family for a reunion. I couldn't go because I was Justa Williams and I was the boss of the Half-Moon ranch, a spread of some thirty thousand deeded acres and some two hundred thousand other acres of government grazing land. I was going on for thirty years old and I'd been running the ranch since I was about eighteen when my father, Howard, had gone down through the death of my mother and a bullet through the lungs. I had two brothers: Ben, who was as wild as a March hare, and Norris, the middle brother, who'd read too many books.

For myself I was tired as hell and needed, badly, to get away from it all, even if it was just to go on a two-week drunk. We were a big organization. What with the ranch and other property and investments our outfit was worth something like two million dollars. And as near as I could figure, I'd been carrying all that load for all those years without much of a break of any kind except for a week's honeymoon with Nora. In short I was tired and I was given out and I was wishing for a relief from all the damn responsibility. If it hadn't been work, it had been a fight or trouble of some kind. Back East, in that year of 1895, the world was starting to get sort of civilized. But along the coastal bend of Texas, in Matagorda County, a man could still get messages from some nameless person threatening to kill him on sight.

I went on into the house and sat down. It was cool in there, a relief from the July heat. It was a long, low, Mexican ranch-style house with red tile on the roof, a fairly big house with thick walls that Nora had mostly designed. The house I'd grown up in, the big house, the house we called ranch headquarters, was about a half a mile away. Both of my brothers still lived there with our dad and a few cooks and maids of all work. But I was tired of work, tired of all of it, tired of listening to folks whining and complaining and expecting me to make it all right. Whatever it was.

And now this message had come. Well, it wasn't any surprise. I'd been threatened before so they weren't getting a man who'd come late in life to being a cherry. I was so damned tired that for a while I just sat there with the message in my hand without much curiosity as to who had sent it.

Lord, the place was quiet. Without Nora's presence and that of my eight-month-old heir, who was generally screaming his head off, the place seemed like it had gone vacant.

For a long time I just sat there, staring at the brief message. I had enemies aplenty but, for the life of me, I couldn't think of any who would send me such a note. Most of them would have come busting through the front door with a shotgun or a pair of revolvers. No, it had to be the work of a gun hired by someone who'd thought I'd done him dirt. And he had to be someone who figured to cause me a good deal of worry in addition to whatever else he had planned for me. It was noontime, but I didn't feel much like eating even though Nora had left Juanita, our cook and maid and maybe the fattest cook and maid in the county, to look after me. She came in and asked me in Spanish what I wanted to eat. I told her nothing and, since she looked so disappointed, I told her she could peel me an apple and fetch it to me. Then I got up and went in my office, where my whiskey was, and poured myself out a good, stiff drink. Most folks would have said it was too hot for hard liquor, but I was not of that mind. Besides, I was mighty glum. Nora hadn't been gone quite a week out of the month's visit she had planned, and already I was mooning around the house and cussing myself for ever giving her permission to go in the first place. That week had given me some idea of how she'd felt when I'd been called away on ranch business of some kind or another and been gone for a considerable time. I'd always thought her complaints had just come from an overwrought female, but I reckoned it had even been lonelier for her. At least now I had my work and was out and about the ranch, while she'd mostly been stuck in the house without a female neighbor nearer than five miles to visit and gossip with.

Of course I could have gone and stayed in the big house, returned to my old ways just as if I were still single. But I was reluctant to do that. For one thing it would have meant eating Buttercup's cooking, which was a chore any sane man would have avoided. But it was considerably more than that; I'd moved out and I had a home and I figured that was the place for me to be. Nora's presence was still there; I could feel it. I could even imagine I could smell the last lingering wisps from her perfume.

Besides that, I figured one or both of my brothers would have some crack to make about not being able to stand my own company or was I homesick for Mommy to come back. We know each other like we knew our own guns and nothing was off limits as far as the joshing went.

But I did want to confer with them about the threatening note. That was family as well as ranch business. There was nobody, neither of my brothers, even with Dad's advice, who was capable of running the ranch, which was the cornerstone of our business. If something were to happen to me we would be in a pretty pickle. Many years before I'd started an upgrading program in our cattle by bringing in Shorthorn cattle from the Midwest, Herefords, whiteface purebreds, to breed to our all-bone, horse-killing, half-crazy-half-wild herd of Longhorns. It had worked so successfully that we now had a purebred herd of our own of Herefords, some five hundred of them, as well as a herd of some five thousand crossbreds that could be handled and worked without wearing out three horses before the noon meal. Which had been the case when I'd inherited herds of pure Longhorns when Howard had turned the ranch over to me.

But there was an art in that crossbreeding and I was the only one who really understood it. You just didn't throw a purebred Hereford bull in with a bunch of crossbred cows and let him do the deciding. No, you had to keep herd books and watch your bloodlines and breed for a certain conformation that would give you the most beef per pound of cow. As a result, our breeding program had produced cattle that we easily sold to the Northern markets for nearly twice what my stubborn neighbors were getting for their cattle.

I figured to go over to the big house and show the note to my brothers and Howard and see what they thought, but I didn't figure to go until after supper. It had always been our custom, even after my marriage, for all of us to gather in the big room that was about half office and half sitting room and sit around discussing the day's events and having a few after-supper drinks. It was also then when, if anybody had any proposals, they could present them to me for my approval. Norris ran the business end of our affairs, but he couldn't make a deal over a thousand dollars without my say-so. Of course that was generally just a formality since his was the better judgment in such matters. But there had to be just one boss and that was me. As I say, a situation I was finding more and more wearisome.

I thought to go up to the house about seven of the evening. Juanita would have fixed my supper and they would have had theirs, and we'd all be relaxed and I could show them the note and get their opinion. Personally, I thought it was somebody's idea of a prank. If you are going to kill a man it ain't real good policy to warn him in advance.

About seven I set out walking toward the big house. It was just coming dusk and there was a nice breeze blowing in from the gulf. I kept three saddle horses in the little corral behind my house, but I could walk the half mile in just about the same time as it would take me to get up a horse and get him saddled and bridled. Besides, the evening was pleasant and I felt the need to stretch my legs.

I let myself into the house through the back door, passed the door to the dining room, and then turned left into the big office. Dad was sitting in his rocking chair near to the door of the little bedroom he occupied. Norris was working at some papers on his side of the big double desk we shared. Ben was in a straight-backed chair he had tilted back against the wall. The whiskey was on the table next to Ben. When I came in the room he said, "Well, well, if it ain't the deserted bridegroom. Taken to loping your mule yet?"

I made a motion as if to kick the chair out from under him and said, "Shut up, Ben. You'd be the one to know about that."

Howard said, "Any word from Nora yet, son?"

I shook my head. "Naw. I told her to go and enjoy herself and not worry about writing me." I poured myself out a drink and then went and sat in a big easy chair that was against the back wall. Norris looked up from his work and said, "Justa, how much higher are you going to let this cattle market go before you sell off some beef?"

"About a week," I said. "Maybe a little longer."

"Isn't that sort of taking a gamble? The bottom could fall out of this market any day."

"Norris, didn't anybody ever tell you that ranching was a gamble?"

"Yes," he said, "I believe you've mentioned that three or four hundred times. But the point is I could use the cash right now. There's a new issue of U.S. treasury bonds that are paying four percent. Those cattle we should be shipping right now are about to reach the point of diminishing returns."

Ben said, "Whatever in the hell that means."

I said, "I'll think it over." I ragged Norris a good deal and got him angry at every good opportunity, but I generally listened when he was talking about money.

After that Ben and I talked about getting some fresh blood in the horse herd. The hard work was done for the year but some of our mounts were getting on and we'd been crossbreeding within the herd too long. I told Ben I thought he ought to think about getting a few good Morgan studs and breeding them in with some of our younger quarter horse mares. For staying power there was nothing like a Morgan. And if you crossed that with the quick speed of a quarter horse you had something that would stay with you all day under just about any kind of conditions.

After that we talked about this and that, until I finally dragged the note out of my pocket. I said, not wanting to make it seem too important, "Got a little love letter this noon. Wondered what ya'll thought about it." I got out of my chair and walked over and handed it to Ben. He read it and then brought all four legs of his chair to the floor with a thump and read it again. He looked over at me. "What the hell! You figure this to be the genuine article?"

I shrugged and went back to my chair. "I don't know," I said. "I wanted to get ya'll's opinion."

Ben got up and handed the note to Norris. He read it and then raised his eyebrows. "How'd you get this?"

"That messenger boy from the telegraph office, Joshua, brought it out to me. Said some man had given him a dollar to bring it out."

"Did you ask him what the man looked like?"

I said drily, "Yes, Norris, I asked him what the man looked like but he said he didn't know. Said all he saw was the dollar."

Norris said, "Well, if it's somebody's idea of a joke it's a damn poor one." He reached back and handed the letter to Howard.

Dad was a little time in reading the note since Norris had to go and fetch his spectacles out of his bedroom. When he'd got them adjusted he read it over several times and then looked at me. "Son, I don't believe this is something you can laugh off. You and this ranch have made considerable enemies through the years. The kind of enemies who don't care if they were right or wrong and the kind of enemies who carry a grudge forever."

"Then why warn me?"

Norris said, "To get more satisfaction out of it. To scare you."

I looked at Dad. He shook his head. "If they know Justa well enough to want to kill him they'll also know he don't scare. No, there's another reason. They must know Justa ain't all that easy to kill. About like trying to corner a cat in a railroad roundhouse. But if you put a man on his guard and keep him on his guard, it's got to eventually take off some of the edge. Wear him down to where he ain't really himself. The same way you buck down a bronc. Let him do all the work against himself."

I said, "So you take it serious, Howard?"

"Yes, sir," he said. "I damn well do. This ain't no prank."

"What shall I do?"

Norris said, "Maybe we ought to run over in our minds the people you've had trouble with in the past who've lived to bear a grudge."

I said, "That's a lot of folks."

Ben said, "Well, there was that little war we had with that Preston family over control of the island."

Howard said, "Yes, but that was one ranch against another."

Norris said, "Yes, but they well knew that Justa was running matters. As does everyone who knows this ranch. So any grudge directed at the ranch is going to be directed right at Justa."

I said, with just a hint of bitterness, "Was that supposed to go with the job, Howard? You didn't explain that part to me."

Ben said, "What about the man in the buggy? He sounds like a likely suspect for such a turn."

Norris said, "But he was crippled."

Ben gave him a sour look. "He's from the border, Norris. You reckon he couldn't hire some gun help?"

Howard said, "Was that the hombre that tried to drive that herd of cattle with tick fever through our range? Those Mexican cattle that hadn't been quarantined?"

Norris said, "Yes, Dad. And Justa made that little man, whatever his name was, drive up here and pay damages."

Ben said, "And he swore right then and there that *he'd* make Justa pay damages."

I said, "For my money it's got something to do with that maniac up in Bandera County that kept me locked up in a root cellar for nearly a week and then tried to have me hung for a crime I didn't even know about."

"But you killed him. And damn near every gun hand he had."

I said, "Yeah, but there's always that daughter of his. And there was a son."

Ben gave me a slight smile. "I thought ya'll was close. I mean *real* close. You and the daughter."

I said, "What we done didn't have anything to do with

anything. And I think she was about as crazy as her father. And, Ben, if you ever mention that woman around Nora, I'm liable to send you one of those notes."

Norris said, "But that's been almost three years ago."

I shook my head. "Time ain't nothing to a woman. They got the patience of an Indian. She'd wait this long just figuring it'd take that much time to forget her."

Norris said skeptically, "That note doesn't look made by a woman's hand."

I said, "It's block lettering, Norris. That doesn't tell you a damn thing. Besides, maybe she hired a gun hand who could write."

Ben said, "I never heard of one."

Howard said, waving the note, "Son, what are you going to do about this?"

I shrugged. "Well, Dad, I don't see where there's anything for me to do right now. I can't shoot a message and until somebody either gets in front of me or behind me or *somewheres,* I don't see what I can do except keep a sharp lookout."

The next day I was about two miles from ranch headquarters, riding my three-year-old bay gelding, down the little wagon track that led to Blessing, when I heard the whine of a bullet passing just over my head, closely followed by the crack of a distant rifle. I never hesitated; I just fell off my horse to the side away from the sound of the rifle. I landed on all fours in the roadbed, and then crawled as quick as I could toward the sound and into the high grass. My horse had run off a little ways, surprised at my unusual dismount. He turned his head to look at me, wondering, I expected, what the hell was going on.

But I was too busy burrowing into that high grass as slow as I could so as not to cause it to ripple or sway or give away my position in any other way to worry about my horse.

I took off my hat on account of its high crown, and then I eased my revolver out of its holster, cocking it as I did. I was carrying a .42/.40 Navy Colt, which is a .40-caliber cartridge chamber on a .42-caliber frame. The .42-caliber frame gave it a good weight in the hand with less barrel deviation, and the .40-caliber bullets it fired would stop anything you hit in the right place. But it still wasn't any match for a rifle at long range, even with the six-inch barrel. My enemy, whoever he was, could just sit there patiently and fire at the slightest movement, and he had to eventually get me because I couldn't lay out there all day. It was only ten of the morning, but already the sun was way up and plenty hot. I could feel a little trickle of sweat running down my nose, but I dared not move to wipe it away for fear even that slight movement could be seen. And I couldn't chance raising my head enough to see for that too would expose my position. All I could do was lay there, staring down at the earth, and wait, knowing that at any second, my bushwhacker could be making his way silently in my direction. He'd have to know, given the terrain, the general location of where I was hiding.

Of course he might have thought he'd hit me, especially from the way I'd just fallen off my horse. I took a cautious look to my left. My horse was still about ten yards away, cropping at the grass along the side of the road. Fortunately, the tied reins had fallen behind the saddle horn and were held there. If I wanted to make a run for it I wouldn't have to spend the time gathering up the reins. The bad part of that was that our horses were taught to ground-rein. When you got off, if you dropped the reins they'd stand there just as if they were tied to a stump. But this way my horse was free to wander off as the spirit might move him. Leaving me afoot whilst being stalked by a man with a rifle.

I tried to remember how close the bullet had sounded over my head and whether or not the assassin might have thought he'd hit me. He had to have been firing upward because there was no other concealment except the high grass. Then I got to thinking I hadn't seen a horse. Well, there were enough little depressions in the prairie that he could have hid a horse some ways back and then come forward on foot and concealed himself in the high grass when he saw me coming.

But how could he have known I was coming? Well, that one wasn't too hard to figure out. I usually went to town at least two or three times a week. If the man had been watching me at all he'd of known that. So then all he'd of had to do was come out every morning and just wait. Sooner or later he was bound to see me coming along, either going or returning.

But I kept thinking about that shot. I'd had my horse in a walk, just slouching along. And God knows, I made a big enough target. In that high grass he could easily have concealed himself close enough for an easy shot, especially if he was a gun hand. The more I thought about it the more I began to think the shooter had been aiming to miss me, to scare me, to wear me down as Howard had said. If the note had come from somebody with an old grudge, they'd *want* me to know who was about to kill me or have me killed. And a bushwhacking rifle shot wasn't all that personal. Maybe the idea was to just keep worrying me until I got to twitching and where I was about a quarter of a second slow. That would be about all the edge a good gun hand would need.

I'd been laying there for what I judged to be a good half hour. Unfortunately I'd crawled in near an ant mound and there was a constant stream of the little insects passing by my hands. Sooner or later one of them was going to sting me. By now I was soaked in sweat and starting to get little cramps from laying so still. I know I couldn't stay there much longer. At any second my horse might take it into his head to go loping back to the barn. As it was he was steadily eating his way further and further from my position.

I made up my mind I was going to have to do something. I cautiously and slowly raised my head until I could just see over the grass. There wasn't anything to see except grass. There was no man, no movement, not even a head of cattle that the gunman might have secreted himself behind.

I took a deep breath and moved, jamming my hat on my head as I did and ramming my gun into its holster. I ran, keeping as low as I could, to my horse. He gave me a startled look, but he didn't spook. Ben trains our horses to expect nearly anything. If they are of a nervous nature we don't keep them.

I reached his left side, stuck my left boot in the stirrup, and swung my right leg just over the saddle. Then, hanging on to his side, I grabbed his right rein with my right hand and pulled his head around until he was pointing up the road. I was holding on to the saddle with my left hand. I kicked him in the ribs as best I could, and got him into a trot and then into a lope going up the road toward town. I tell you, it was hell hanging on to his side. I'd been going a-horseback since I could walk, but I wasn't no trick rider and the position I was in made my horse run sort of sideways so that his gait was rough and awkward.

But I hung on him like that for what I judged to be a quarter of a mile and out of rifle shot. Only then did I pull myself up into the saddle and settle myself into a normal position to ride a horse. Almost immediately I pulled up and turned into the saddle to look back. Not a thing was stirring, just innocent grass waving slightly in the light breeze that had sprung up.

I shook my head, puzzled. Somebody was up to something, but I was damned if I could tell what. If they were trying to make me uneasy they were doing a good job of it. And the fact that I was married and had a wife and child to care for, and a hell of a lot more reason to live than when I was a single man, was a mighty big influence in my worry. It could be that the person behind the threats was aware of that and was taking advantage of it. If such was the case, it made me think more and more that it was the work of the daughter of the maniac in Bandera that had tried in several ways to end my life. It was the way a woman would think because she would know about such things. I couldn't visualize the man in the buggy understanding that a man with loved ones will cling harder to life for their sake than a man with nothing else to lose except his own hide.

J.R. ROBERTS
THE
GUNSMITH

___THE GUNSMITH #118:	SCARLET FURY	0-515-10691-7/$3.50
___THE GUNSMITH #119:	ARIZONA AMBUSH	0-515-10710-7/$3.50
___THE GUNSMITH #120:	THE VENGEANCE TRAIL	0-515-10735-2/$3.50
___THE GUNSMITH #121:	THE DEADLY DERRINGER	0-515-10755-7/$3.50
___THE GUNSMITH #122:	THE STAGECOACH KILLERS	0-515-10792-1/$3.50
___THE GUNSMITH #123:	FIVE AGAINST DEATH	0-515-10810-3/$3.50
___THE GUNSMITH #124:	MUSTANG MAN	0-515-10834-0/$3.50
___THE GUNSMITH #125:	THE GODFATHER	0-515-10851-0/$3.50
___THE GUNSMITH #126:	KILLER'S GOLD	0-515-10867-7/$3.50
___THE GUNSMITH #127:	GHOST TOWN	0-515-10882-0/$3.50
___THE GUNSMITH #128:	THE CALIENTE GOLD ROBBERY	0-515-10903-7/$3.99
___THE GUNSMITH #129:	GOLDEN GATE KILLERS	0-515-10931-2/$3.99
___THE GUNSMITH #130:	THE ROAD TO TESTIMONY	0-515-10957-6/$3.99
___THE GUNSMITH #131:	THE WITNESS (Nov. 1992)	0-515-10982-7/$3.99
___THE GUNSMITH #132:	THE GREAT RIVERBOAT RACE (Dec. 1992)	0-515-10999-1/$3.99

For Visa, MasterCard and American Express orders ($15 minimum) call: **1-800-631-8571**

Check book(s). Fill out coupon. Send to:
BERKLEY PUBLISHING GROUP
390 Murray Hill Pkwy., Dept. B
East Rutherford, NJ 07073

NAME _____
ADDRESS _____
CITY _____
STATE _____ ZIP _____

PLEASE ALLOW 6 WEEKS FOR DELIVERY.
PRICES ARE SUBJECT TO CHANGE
WITHOUT NOTICE.

POSTAGE AND HANDLING:
$1.75 for one book, 75¢ for each additional. Do not exceed $5.50.

BOOK TOTAL	$____
POSTAGE & HANDLING	$____
APPLICABLE SALES TAX (CA, NJ, NY, PA)	$____
TOTAL AMOUNT DUE	$____

PAYABLE IN US FUNDS.
(No cash orders accepted.)

206d

If you enjoyed this book, subscribe now and get...

TWO FREE

A $7.00 VALUE—

If you would like to read more of the very best, most exciting, adventurous, action-packed Westerns being published today, you'll want to subscribe to True Value's Western Home Subscription Service.

Each month the editors of True Value will select the 6 very best Westerns from America's leading publishers for special readers like you. You'll be able to preview these new titles as soon as they are published, *FREE* for ten days with no obligation!

TWO FREE BOOKS

When you subscribe, we'll send you your first month's shipment of the newest and best 6 Westerns for you to preview. With your first shipment, two of these books will be yours as our introductory gift to you absolutely *FREE* (a $7.00 value), regardless of what you decide to do. If you like them, as much as we think you will, keep all six books but pay for just 4 at the low subscriber rate of just $2.75 each. If you decide to return them, keep 2 of the titles as our gift. No obligation.

Special Subscriber Savings

When you become a True Value subscriber you'll save money several ways. First, all regular monthly selections will be billed at the low subscriber price of just $2.75 each. That's at least a savings of $4.50 each month below the publishers price. Second, there is never any shipping, handling or other hidden charges—*Free home delivery*. What's more there is no minimum number of books you must buy, you may return any selection for full credit and you can cancel your subscription at any time. A TRUE VALUE!

A special offer for people who enjoy reading the best Westerns published today.

WESTERNS!

NO OBLIGATION

Mail the coupon below

To start your subscription and receive 2 FREE WESTERNS, fill out the coupon below and mail it today. We'll send your first shipment which includes 2 FREE BOOKS as soon as we receive it.

Mail To: **True Value Home Subscription Services, Inc. P.O. Box 5235
120 Brighton Road, Clifton, New Jersey 07015-5235**

YES! I want to start reviewing the very best Westerns being published today. Send me my first shipment of 6 Westerns for me to preview FREE for 10 days. If I decide to keep them, I'll pay for just 4 of the books at the low subscriber price of $2.75 each; a total $11.00 (a $21.00 value). Then each month I'll receive the 6 newest and best Westerns to preview Free for 10 days. If I'm not satisfied I may return them within 10 days and owe nothing. Otherwise I'll be billed at the special low subscriber rate of $2.75 each; a total of $16.50 (at least a $21.00 value) and save $4.50 off the publishers price. There are never any shipping, handling or other hidden charges. I understand I am under no obligation to purchase any number of books and I can cancel my subscription at any time, no questions asked. In any case the 2 FREE books are mine to keep.

Name _____

Street Address _____ Apt. No. _____

City _____ State _____ Zip Code _____

Telephone _____

Signature _____
(if under 18 parent or guardian must sign)

10957

Terms and prices subject to change. Orders subject
to acceptance by True Value Home Subscription
Services, Inc.

"1991 GOLDEN SPUR AWARD WINNER"

Golden Spur Awards have been given to such greats as Nelson Nye, Louis L'Amour and Elmer Kelton. Awarded by the Western Writers of America, it recognizes literature and art that best portray the American West.

JOURNAL OF THE GUN YEARS
Richard Matheson

EVERY HERO HAS HIS SECRETS.
BUT SOME LEGENDS NEVER DIE.

Marshal Clay Halser was a legend in the Southwest. Back east they told tall tales about Clay Halser, the Civil War Veteran who cleaned up the West. He was a fugitive wanted for murder. An outlaw on the run. An acquaintance of Cullen Baker and Wild Bill Hickok. And in spite of his past, he became one of the greatest lawmen of all time. But behind the myth—in his own private journal—lies the true story of Marshal Clay Halser...

__ 0-425-13207-2/$4.50

For Visa, MasterCard and American Express orders ($15 minimum) call: 1-800-631-8571

FOR MAIL ORDERS: CHECK BOOK(S). FILL OUT COUPON. SEND TO:

BERKLEY PUBLISHING GROUP
390 Murray Hill Pkwy., Dept. B
East Rutherford, NJ 07073

NAME_____

ADDRESS_____

CITY_____

STATE_____ ZIP_____

PLEASE ALLOW 6 WEEKS FOR DELIVERY.
PRICES ARE SUBJECT TO CHANGE WITHOUT NOTICE.

POSTAGE AND HANDLING:
$1.75 for one book, 75¢ for each additional. Do not exceed $5.50.

BOOK TOTAL	$ ____
POSTAGE & HANDLING	$ ____
APPLICABLE SALES TAX (CA, NJ, NY, PA)	$ ____
TOTAL AMOUNT DUE	$ ____

PAYABLE IN US FUNDS.
(No cash orders accepted.)